CU00905895

For the past ten years Kay Jaybee has lived a nomadic existence across the British Isles, collecting stories as she travels. Kay is a regular contributor to the erotica web site *Oysters and Chocolate*. A number of her short stories have featured in anthologies published by *Xcite Press, Black Lace, Mammoth Publications* and *Cleis Press,* including *Best Women's Erotica 2007* and *2008.*

THE COLLECTOR

Kay Jaybee

THE COLLECTOR

AUSTIN MACAULEY

A CIP catalogue record for this title is
available from the British Library.

ISBN 978 1 905609 19 2

www.austinmacauley.com

First Published (2008)
Austin & Macauley Publishers Ltd.
25 Canada Square
Canary Wharf
London
E14 5LB

Printed & Bound in Great Britain

DEDICATION

To S, with love.

Acknowledgements.

My love and thanks to S and my family for their help and support. I am also grateful to AMH, BH, DB, RT, LW, NB and GM, for their encouragement and friendship, despite their occasional bewilderment at my choice of career.

Special mention must be made to both Samantha Sade and Jordan LaRousse of *Oysters and Chocolate.com*, who gave me my first real break into the world of web publication, and to Violet Blue, who backed my story *Jen and Tim*, and saw it through to publication in her anthology *'Lips Like Sugar.'* Since that time, Violet has been kind enough to include several of my tales in her books, including *Tied to the Kitchen Sink*, which not only features in the anthology *'Lust'*, but has also been made into a pod-cast on her *Open Source Sex* web site.

Finally, I must thank my sources of inspiration. You know who you are.

CONTENTS

Page

1.	New Territory	15
2.	Jay	24
3.	Learning	26
4.	Studio Girl	29
5.	Sweets	35
6.	The Experiment	41
7.	Car Love	43
8.	Late Developer	45
9.	Treasure	49
10.	Executive School	57
11.	Tequila	69
12.	Bad Behaviour The Candle Holder	78
13.	Untouched	82
14.	Watching	89
15.	Crushed	95
16.	Break Time	99
17.	Cupboard Lust	103
18.	Dark Knight	105
19.	Van	116
20.	Alone	120
	Epilogue	122

CHAPTER ONE

As the pile of manuscripts on my desk continues to grow, I am continually surprised at how easy it is to write this stuff. There is just so much material out there.

Hungrily, I listen to the erotic acrobatics of total strangers and commit them to paper, usually whilst in a café or coffee house. There is something deliciously naughty about sitting innocently writing in a crisp, white notebook, sipping coffee and eating pastries amongst the town's shopping population. I often wonder if my fellow coffee drinkers imagine me to be writing extensive shopping lists, children's stories perhaps, maybe a little light romantic fiction. Not highly charged tales of sexual submission. Not bondage and sexual slavery. I just don't look that type, which just goes to show you can never tell. In fact, my rather innocent looking appearance is a very useful tool in my quest for stories of consensual depravity. I don't look like a threat. People can tell me anything – and they frequently do.

In view of this confession of general 'ordinariness,' I feel that the first story should provide some proof to the reader that they'll not be disappointed by what follows, that I am able to, as it were, put my money where my mouth is.

Occasionally, when my sources run dry, I do some in-depth research of my own; take some direct action. This usually entails a trip away from my residence in Oxford to London, where I take a short lease on a flat, adopt a more suitable persona (I should have been on the stage), and explore areas of potential inspiration.

The last time I went into the city was particularly rewarding; he was someone truly worth writing about.

I think it's only fair to retell the story from his point of view.

New Territory

It hadn't seemed significant when he'd noticed which page she'd left the colour supplement open at. Perhaps it wasn't; coincidences happened all the time. No. He saw now that it was no accident; she had been trying to tell him something.

She was sat at the corner table at the very back of the coffee shop. The armchairs were rather comfortable in that area; he always tried to sit there. As he worked his way along the queue, collecting an almond danish and ordering a frighteningly large black coffee, he watched her. Sitting slightly upright, she was partially obscured by a copy of *The Observer*, her long booted legs curled under the armchair, her red hair framing her small face. She was sipping a cappuccino. He couldn't help but smile as he watched her develop a foam moustache, and quite uncaring, lick it off with her tongue. He looked away and concentrated on his tray as he pushed towards the till. It was disconcerting to find himself aroused by such a simple act. He paid, collected his sugar and turned to find a seat.

He could have sat anywhere, but she already felt like an itch needing a scratch. He had to talk to her. So what if she told him to piss off; he was only going to ask if he could share the table.

He asked and she inclined her head, not glancing up for more than a second; so he sat. This was new territory for him; he'd never felt such a need to say something, anything. He was the good looking one, the one who never had to say anything. They came to him. Now the silence seemed to be an oppressive presence in itself, like a whole extra person in the room who wasn't saying anything.

This was ridiculous. He picked up his own paper, folded it to the business pages and took a bite of his pastry, trying not to mind that icing sugar was dusting his new black jacket.

She'd finished her drink. He flirted with the idea of offering to buy her a new one, but quickly dismissed it. He hadn't even said hello to her. So why did he feel that time was running out? Why did he feel a strange sensation of panic that she was going to leave before he'd heard her voice?

As she unfolded her legs and tided her paper, she picked up her large brown rucksack, pulled out some keys and stood in front of him. He looked up into her face. He was being assessed. It was a strange sensation; he usually did the assessing.

'Are you coming then?' She spoke very softly, her green eyes shining with a sort of inner power.

He was about to ask if she was sure, but she'd already turned around and was heading for the door.

He was well aware of the fact that he was probably about to make a total fool of himself, but he followed anyway. She walked very quickly; striding along in impossibly high heels. It hadn't occurred to him until that point that she might be a hooker. What if she was? He'd just walk away. Maybe?

He followed as she turned down a gap between two shops. There was a flight of black iron stairs that led up to a flat above one of them. She stopped. 'Two things,' she undid her leather jacket as she spoke, hitching her scarf open to reveal a delicate neck completely unadorned by jewellery. 'One; I do not do this for money, and two; I am not inviting you in for coffee.'

He nodded, undid his own coat, and followed her up the steps.

The hall was very narrow. It led to a modest kitchen diner, where she placed her paper, spread open, on the table. Sorting out the magazine, she opened it up as if she was going to settle down to read, but then didn't.

He hadn't got as far as making small talk. In fact he hadn't even got as far as attempting to make small talk, when she took him by the hand and led him into the small living room, sitting him down on the small maroon sofa. She knelt and, placing a restraining hand on his leg, undid his shoes and placed them neatly to one side. Then she did the same with his socks.

That was when his body stopped making his hands clammy and his heart beat faster, and sent all excess blood directly to his dick. He'd known he'd been half way to a hard-on already, but now there was no disguising the fact.

'You would be a Coldplay man, or maybe Keane? Dido?' She stood by the tiny stereo.

'Dido.'

She nodded, pressed buttons and waited as the haunting notes built up to the opening number.

He should do something. He tried to stand, but she just raised her hand and he quickly sat down again. Maybe this wasn't his show; new territory.

She was standing about two metres away from him. Her jacket had already hit the floor, and he caught his breath as he watched her long slim fingers begin to undo the buttons of her white blouse. She looked straight at him the whole time; each movement in time to the music, and he found himself wishing that he'd chosen something with a faster pace.

His throat felt dry as she revealed a beautiful cream bra. He could see her nipples, hard and dark, pressing against the thin lace. He started to wonder how wet she would be, and then stopped himself. If he started to think like that he'd shoot his load before he even got his trousers off. He'd never felt so unsure of himself as she stepped out of her suede skirt, letting it drop over her boots.

Now he desperately wanted to touch. The smooth shoulders that had just been revealed cried out to be caressed. Anyway, he was becoming uncomfortable; his cock was digging into his waistband, as it struggled to force itself from his jeans unaided. He should say something, but he didn't want to break the spell.

She stopped. He stared at the floor by her feet and worked his eyes slowly upwards. He tried to imprint the vision before him onto his brain inch by inch. High heeled boots; beige. Soft pale flesh emerging from lace hold-ups; cream. Slightly see-through French knickers; cream. *'Keep going. Try to drag your eyes away from the neat silhouetted triangle your eyes can just make out'*, he thought to himself as he swallowed, continuing his inventory. A flat stomach with a neat belly button. A cream lace bra encasing neatly rounded breasts which poked tantalisingly over the top. He took a deep breath and looked at her face. Small features, bobbed red hair, deep green eyes which gave absolutely nothing away.

The room was charged with electricity; so enticing, so dangerous. She moved forward and gestured for him to stand. He hadn't been able to suppress his groan as he stood. His stomach felt strange and his dick ached to be freed from its confinement.

He waited, doing nothing. He didn't know what to do, so he let her take control; keep control. She took his belt first; pulling it out very slowly, loop by loop. She slid the brown leather between her fingers. 'I like belts.' That was all she said, but he suddenly realised that he wanted to hit her with it. He needed to yank down her knickers and punish her for being perfect.

She undid his shirt next. His arms hung against his sides. He wanted to touch so badly, but he sensed that that would screw things up. This ritual, so painfully slow, was possibly the most erotic thing he'd ever seen.

When she kissed his nipples he yelled. It was like someone placing an ice cube down his front on a scolding day; wonderful, but totally agonising. Her mouth worked its way across his tanned chest. His hands automatically went to hold her face, but she took hold of them and kept them firmly by his sides, whilst her teeth began to graze the skin above his jeans waistband.

He'd read about women who could undo jean flies with just their teeth, but had dismissed them as pornographic fantasy. It appeared that he was wrong. It took a very hard tug of his jeans however to get them right down. His cock had swollen so much that it was now stuck with its shiny red head sticking out of the top of his white briefs. He would never forget that moment, it was the first time he saw her smile as he flushed with embarrassment at his obvious need for her body.

'No, don't worry. I think he looks gorgeous,' and with that she yanked off his underwear and stared with sheer lust, admiring him standing to attention before her. Never before had he felt so utterly naked; or so totally observed.

Her eyes flicked to a small table by the sofa. A condom sat waiting. He nodded in silent understanding, hope flooding through him.

She had begun to quiver then. Perhaps she was real after all and not some incredible apparition with iron clad self-control. He watched amazed, as she came in front of him, without a single finger being laid on her. Power. She'd made him want her, and that alone had got her off.

It hadn't ended. He feared for a split second that that might have been enough for her, and his services were no longer required; but her hands came up to him now and she'd pulled him close to her. In a quiet whisper of pleading she said, 'I seem to have been rather naughty,' she glanced at the belt. 'I wonder if you would mind administering the punishment I am obviously due.'

He swallowed again then as he nodded. Had she known that was what he wanted to do to her? His cock stirred on its own; he badly needed relief. He'd never had to wait so long for his own satisfaction before, and he wasn't sure he could trust himself not to come all over her as they stood there. The girl was psychic; she had to be, for suddenly, as he picked up his belt, she fell to her knees and, in a totally unexpected move, engulfed him between her red lips.

It was like being encased in the softest silk and pumped to death. She was unquestioningly an expert. As her tongue lapped his tip, whilst her throat surrounded him, he ran the belt between his fingers. The pressure began to build and he felt as though he would explode. His head swam and he clamped his eyes closed, placing his hands on her shoulders to steady himself. As his spunk hammered down her throat he threw his head back and roared. He felt light headed, drunk, and yet now he was free of his initial frustration, the realisation of the shift of control flooded through him.

She was still on her knees when he opened his eyes. White droplets of his load trickled from the corner of her mouth. She did nothing about them; just let them run down her chin and her neck. He watched the sticky drops lodge into her cleavage. That was self-control; he would have had to wipe them off. Her eyes looked up at him through her fringe. She said nothing, but her thoughts were so loud they almost echoed around the room. '*Now I've been really bad haven't I?*'

It was his turn. He pointed to the arm of the sofa and watched, his state of arousal already returning, as she positioned herself so that her upper body lay across the arm, whilst her legs remained on the floor. Her fabric covered arse filled his vision. He adored it. Ripe, round and firm. His hands stroked the flimsy material. His finger tips teased beneath the leg holes, making her skin jump beneath his touch as he slithered the fragile knickers down to just below her buttocks before running a single finger down her butt-crack.

He couldn't wait any longer. She was just too perfect. He looped the belt in half and wrapped it a little way around his wrist before aiming it against her skin, first with a gentle leather caress, then a smack, before building up a rhythm. Faster and faster; harder and harder. Each stroke of the belt hit an alternate cheek, quickly creating a striped effect across her pale flesh.

She'd cried out at first, but then began to stifle her reaction into a cushion. She bit down hard, effectively gagging herself and deflecting the beautiful pain.

He felt even more turned on than before; if only she would beg him to stop. He'd struck her three more times before something in her snapped and she cried out. 'Please Sir', she'd shouted, 'Please stop. Fuck me Sir. Fuck me now.'

That was when it had really started.

He pulled on the condom, grabbed her hips, lifted her slightly, and thrust into her from behind. As he rocked in and out of her tight cunt, his hands digging into the recently spoilt flesh, her breathing had become shallow. She was close now, desperate perhaps. Swiftly he pulled out and tugged her to her feet. She swayed as the blood that had run to her head drained back through her body.

She watched him transfixed as, holding her upright with one hand, he licked one finger and placed it lightly onto her hard clit. The mewls that had been issuing from her lips became a groan of near satisfaction as she grabbed his hand and held it firmly over her pussy, rubbing herself off until, at last, she sank to her feet, shaking as her orgasm washed over her.

He knelt and unzipped her boots, tenderly kissing each inch of skin as it appeared, until he reached her tiny feet and then kissed them too.

She had begun to shiver, and for the first time he noticed that the flat wasn't that warm. Scooping her slight body into his arms, he led her through the open bedroom door. Dropping her onto the coffee coloured duvet, he stood admiring her for a second before climbing astride her. Sitting with his cock resting on her stomach, he leant forward and took her right nipple between his lips and began to nibble it with his teeth.

He could feel her stomach tighten beneath him as a moan caught in her throat. He wanted to take his time; feast on the delicious tits in front of him, but he knew that he only had so long before he would break, before the feel of her velvet body enveloping him was again essential to his very existence.

He sucked, licked and bit her breasts until her sighs had turned to urgent growls. 'Oh God, I can feel you. It's as if every time you lick my tits you are licking my cunt.'

It was the longest sentence she had spoken since they'd met, and it had more effect on him than anything that had happened so far. He felt a strange surge of power that he had made this enigmatic woman feel that way. He sat on the edge of the bed and, silent once more, she climbed astride him, consuming his thick shaft between her legs. He forced a hand between them, rubbing her engorged clit as she came around him, her cries forcing him to spunk into her in a seemingly endless rush of relief.

After that she held him. He was vaguely aware that it felt good to be held. The usual stranglehold of post-coital suffocation wasn't flooding through him. It was as if they both understood the situation for exactly what it was; so being held and holding was fine.

'You'd like a shower?' she asked, her head to one side.

'Please.' He followed her into a tiny room which contained nothing but a shower and a toilet. She reached into the glass cubicle and pressed a button, unleashing a steaming jet of hot water.

It seemed natural to shower together. As he soaped her breasts he saw that this was the end; that if he wanted to know what she tasted like then this was his last chance. He lowered himself to his knees, and in the confined space, eased her legs apart, before darting his tongue between them.

He lapped up her sweet juice as the water crashed around them. He was quickly rewarded by her bucking against his tongue, as she grabbed his sodden hair to steady herself.

Once back on her feet she looked at him as if assessing him once more. She kissed him twice, once on the mouth and once on the cheek. Then, without a word, she pointed to a plush white towel hanging on the rack.

He understood, and in a way he was grateful. No explanations, no excuses; it had just come to an end.

He tracked down his clothes and dressed without haste. In the kitchen he pulled on his jacket, and glanced at the article she'd lain out to read later. He might easily have missed it, but he didn't.

As he sat back in the coffee shop, sipping a much needed black coffee, he opened the colour supplement from the newspaper he'd just purchased.

There she was. An article about the growing trend in woman's erotica greeted him, alongside which was a small, slightly grainy photograph of a writer. It claimed her name was Jen. He suspected that was not the case. It simply didn't suit her.

He smiled. So, he'd been screwed in the interests of research. Seemed like a good reason. He thought perhaps that would be one story he didn't need to read though, for he knew he would remember it always. In fact he was going to remember later at home; vividly in the comfort of his own bedroom, or maybe even in the shower.

CHAPTER TWO

The majority of the stories I have collected are from total strangers. Find the right angle and they seem to relish telling their inner-most secrets. There is a piquant delight in sharing a lurid confidence with someone you don't know, and are unlikely to see ever again, especially someone who might immortalise your adventure in print.

When I met Jay, on the bus from Five Mile Drive to St Giles in Oxford, and saw her blurred eyes looking into the distance, a tired but satisfied smile playing at the corner of her mouth, I instinctively knew she had a story to tell. I just hoped she wasn't too hung over or too stoned to tell me about it.

Jay

She couldn't back out now. This was it, the only chance she would ever have to live out the wild fantasy her mind continually replayed into the small hours of the night.

She nodded, her long black hair falling across her rounded face, hiding a nervous smile. A tall girl took her hand and led her into the ladies cloakroom, away from the buzz of the club. Jay caught her breath as she took in the scene. The action was already underway.

Pressed against the mirrored wall, arms placed high behind her spiky red hair, a fantastically curvaceous girl had her eyes tightly closed. Kneeling before her, an eager petite woman was licking between her spread legs, soft fingers teasing the skin above sheer silk hold-ups. Jay took in the round exposed globes squeezed out seductively above the willing captive's startlingly bright green basque. She didn't need telling what to do. Jay's tongue was quickly lapping at the right nipple like a hungry cat, while her escort greedily attacked the left.

The pace quickened and the nameless girl let out a body racking cry as she bucked away from the mirror, leaving a smeared sweaty outline against the glass. She fell forwards, pulling her attendants down with her.

In the tangle of smooth arms and legs, Jay felt all the hands fall onto her. So, she was to be next. As she was positioned onto all fours, Jay prepared herself to dispel the myth that it is better to give rather than to receive…

CHAPTER THREE

It was in a small conservatory attached to a coffee shop near Carfax, that I overhead the makings of my next story. I had no need to earn the trust of the rather severe middle-aged gentleman who was sat at a table nearby. He was sat explaining to an equally stuffy looking blonde woman how his latest student (apparently a graduate of somewhere unpalatably red-brick), was responding to his particular brand of adult education. I simply had to listen.

Quickly picking up on the tone of their conversation, I knocked over my drink by "mistake", apologised to the staff, and moved to a table closer to the conversation. Taking out my notebook, I pretended to be engrossed in what I was writing – which I was. They had no way of knowing I was recording their conversation in short hand. I doubt if they even noticed me at all.

Learning

'I have been a very naughty boy again haven't I.' A baseball cap brim hid the sorrowful bowed face.

'Yes, I see that you have. You are well aware that you are not allowed to do that without my express permission.'

'I'm sorry Sir. I couldn't help myself.' Blonde hair peaked out from under the cap. The blue hoodie was rucked up at the waist and a pair of jeans and stark white boxer shorts were positioned around the miscreant's ankles. 'I needed to so badly.'

The room was bare except for a small wooden chair and a desk set in its very centre. The floor boards creaked as Sir came towards the figure perched meekly on the edge of the chair. The cane snapped through the silence as it rapped hard against the corners of the desk. The boy jumped, but still didn't look up.

'I'm sure I don't have to remind you of the punishment you're due.' The lack of emotion in his voice belied the bulge which had become clearly visible through his trousers.

'No Sir.' The bowed head lifted slightly. Deep blue eyes watched the cane as it continually flicked against the side of the desk.

'You will take up your position.' Sir swallowed down the desire he felt rising within him at the prospect of punishing his beloved student. His voice remained steady as the young man rose shakily to his feet and turned across the chair, proffering his bare arse.

Sir pushed the hoodie up further, revealing the small of the boys back above the extraordinary pale, but obviously previously whipped buttocks. He traced the exposed crack with the end of his cane, making his target quiver beneath his touch.

The first stroke hit the right cheek, causing his willing victim to yell out in protest, as another harder stroke connected with the other cheek.

'There is no point in screaming young man. You knew the penalty. Ten strokes on your bare bum.'

Tears shone on the pale face as the eighth lash met its goal. On the ninth stroke his head drooped further over the chair, causing his long blonde hair to cascade out from the fallen baseball cap.

Ten.

Sir stopped and laid his cane down. 'Stay where you are.' He quickly divested himself of his trousers and pants and slipped on a condom. He pulled the red bum sharply forwards and impaled himself inside the winking velvet hole, groaning as his pupil simultaneously pushed backwards onto the hard shaft.

Sobbing with pain and lust, the blonde's tear streaked face bawled out. 'Fuck me Sir, Fuck me harder!'

'You are a dirty slut young man!'

'Yes Sir. I am Sir. Fuck me harder Sir."

The master paused. 'I didn't hear you say please Bitch.'

'Please Sir. Please fuck me harder Sir.'

'You asked for it!' Sir cried as he scraped the occupied chair against the floor, such was the violence of his thrusts. Sweat prickled across both their backs as Sir pushed himself to the limit before finally shuddering his release into his protégé's arsehole.

Sir hastily withdrew. 'You shouldn't have made me do that you know.' He wrapped the spent condom into his hanky and threw it into the corner of the room. 'Let me see if you are obeying my other rules.'

The boy stood up slowly and, steadying himself on the chair, kicked away the clothing from around his ankles. Then he pulled off his hoodie to reveal what was beneath.

'Good boy.' The master walked around his pupil admiring the sight before him. The reddened arse; the tight abused anus; the fine slender back and shoulder blades; the stomach without an ounce of excess fat and neatly defined muscles.

The bindings around the pupil's chest were tightly in place. They had begun to become camouflaged against his flesh now he'd worn them for so long.

The strap-on, again carefully selected to match the pale skin tone, hung, forever erect, just off centre, showing evidence of his weakness in continuing to masturbate as a woman despite his master's strict orders to the contrary.

That was why the pupil visited this classroom. To learn. To learn how to behave as Sir would wish and, if he was honest, as he truly desired. And he desired it very much indeed.

CHAPTER FOUR

Now and again it is refreshing to come across a story that has been fuelled by genuine affection, not just lust; although there seems to have been plenty of that too.

Studio Girl

The clothes rack, bedecked with empty hangers had apparently always stood in the corner of the studio. It looked out of place amongst the half painted canvases that lined the walls, and had never had any clothes hanging on it to the best of my knowledge. 'It comes in useful now and again', he'd said when I asked the reason for its presence. As no more information was forth coming I carried on with my careful dusting of the flower pot covered window sills.

I had been cleaning for Max for almost four months. It wasn't glamorous employment, but a much needed way to make extra cash whilst working on my degree. My friends had laughed when I took the job, but I didn't care. It paid better than cleaning offices or working in a fast food shop and, apart from the mind-numbingly dull task of polishing the vast laminate floor every fortnight, it was neither time-consuming nor arduous.

Then of course, there was the scenery. The paintings were, even to my uneducated eye, fantastic. Strong, bold strokes, which seemed to show nothing until you studied them closely. As you stared, the muted hues would run together to make images which somehow always managed to suit my mood. If I'm honest though, even if I had hated every picture I would have stayed. Even if the wages were halved and the work involved sweeping the floor with a toothbrush,

I would have stayed. Max's giant athletic frame was worth watching anytime. Just looking at his calm face, which despite the intensity of some of his work, never seemed to show any flicker of emotion, kept me coming back. I was mesmerised by him, like a rabbit trapped in a car's headlights.

His effect on me was quite alarming. One look and I could feel my face redden, and my nipples would quickly harden at the sound of his gentle Scottish burr. I found myself taking longer and longer to do the simplest of tasks just so I could stay in his presence and dream erotic fantasies about him; or more specifically, about us.

I would go home each afternoon and get cross with myself for being so pathetic, before pleasuring myself across the foot of my bed, the image of his paint spattered torso burnt across my mind. Twice my age, twice divorced, he had no interest in me apart from my ability to clean his lavatory. I was making a fool of myself and it had to stop.

Last week though, everything changed. Now I know exactly what the clothes rack is for.

It was time to polish the floor. I'd put it off all week, but there was no way I could avoid the back breaking work any longer. As the hot sun reflected through the studio's huge light enhancing windows, I could see the smears of countless footprints made by Max's bare feet as he strode purposely around.

I carefully moved all the canvases and easels to one side of the room, before resigning myself to the task, and lowered down onto my hands and knees with a cloth and a tub of wax. After about half an hour of polishing I could no longer feel my knees, and the sweat was beginning to run down my back. I felt sticky and uncomfortable in my tight t-shirt, and the headscarf, which swept my thick curls back out of my eyes, felt prickly in the heat. I straightened up and turned the ceiling fan onto a faster speed. It was so quiet. Max had gone out, looking ill at ease in a shirt and tie, on one of his hated and frequent trips to try and convince an art gallery to exhibit his work.

I was all alone and realised that there was absolutely no need to be so hot. Pulling off my yellow top made me feel so much better that I thought I should take off my jeans as well. After all, who would know? Throwing my discarded clothes onto an old, paint spattered, wooden chair, I cranked on the radio and went back to the floor. Soon I was absorbed in the music and working steadily across the wood. I didn't hear the door open, and was unaware of the soft bare foot falls across the floor. I have no idea how long I was being watched as I knelt there. If I hadn't had a sudden sensation of not being alone, then perhaps he would have just stood there until I'd finished.

My cheeks flushed scarlet as I confronted my unexpected audience, and I began to babble, 'I was hot, I um, I just thought...' Realisation of my almost naked state hit me in a rush, and I rushed over to my clothes. I felt such a fool as I struggled to turn my t-shirt the right way around so I could at least be semi-decent.

His speed of movement took me unawares. 'Don't,' he spoke with deadly soft command, his hand restraining me in the act of dressing. As he looked at me I couldn't decide if he was going to sack me on the spot or ravish me. I hoped like hell it would be the latter.

No one spoke. He put my top back on the heap of clothes and turned me round so I faced the half cleaned floor. Max pointed, the message was clear. I returned to my work, shaking slightly, my mind racing as I felt his eyes on my arse. My flimsy white knickers seemed even more revealing than I remembered, and I made little progress across the wood as my imagination wandered all over the place. The music stopped mid-song as he clicked the radio off. The only remaining sound was the soft rub of my cloth on the smooth floor.

'Stay still,' he whispered into my ear as he crawled, cat like, up behind me. On my hands and knees I felt his weight against me, his denim encased dick pushing hard into my bum as he kissed my neck.

Despite the beautiful sensations his mouth was producing I simply could not keep still. His weight was too much and I collapsed onto the floor, my hot breasts flinching as they hit the cool wood. Max's calloused hands began to examine me as I lay there. I felt as if I was a fresh piece of clay just waiting to be formed into a work of art. His fingers lingered tantalisingly across the top of my knicker's waistband.

I felt light headed, unreal, and my head buzzed with every sensation. Max gently began to slip my knickers down my legs, and I gasped at the touch of his tongue trailing slowly between my butt cheeks. He reached my anus and began to poke his tongue urgently into the hole, forcing me to moan with long pent-up frustration.

This sound seemed to be all the reassurance Max needed, and he swiftly turned me over, removing my bra, and tugging off the head scarf so that my hair curled around my shoulders. Although he remained silent, the intensity in his eyes told me all I needed to know; this was a meeting of mutual lust.

Slipping a hand into mine, he led me to the corner of the room which housed the clothes rack. Leaning towards me, he whispered in a throaty voice, 'Can I tie you up? I am sure you would look fantastic. Will you trust me?'

I nodded, unsure of exactly what he had planned, but knowing that right now I would take any attention he was willing to give. I waited, the tension growing within me, as he fetched some artist's cord and some rags from the chaos of his desk. Positioning me in front of the rack with his usual economy of movement, he raised one arm at a time, gently wrapping each wrist in a scrap of fabric before tying them to the cold bar, pushing the redundant hangers to each side.

Unable to move, the restraints only served to turn me on further, and suddenly my need to feel him inside me became an almost physical pain. Max stood back and admired his work. His breathing had become audible as he struggled between his desire to take in every inch of his creation, and the stirrings of his hidden shaft.

He took a small paintbrush from the closest easel and ran the fine hairs through his fingers. I shuddered as he approached, imagining how the soft fine bristles would feel as they tickled my skin. The cry I uttered as he began to circle the brush around my pale nipples echoed around the cleared space of the studio. Each slow swipe across my swollen breasts felt like an electric shock. He kept on, stroke after stroke, for what seemed like hours, as if he was carefully glazing a statue.

Just as I thought I couldn't handle anymore, my whimpers becoming increasingly frantic, he stopped and stepped back. I could have cried. Max bent down and kissed each breast and I was swept over the edge, my legs shaking and my arms pulling involuntarily against my bonds.

All the time, Max watched. I couldn't imagine how he was staying so controlled. As my orgasm subsided, all I could think about was having another one.   Max obviously had similar intentions for me as he took up the torturous brush once again. Dusting the bristles around my wrists, down my arms and across my back, he systematically managed to turn each area of my body into a new erogenous zone. I wanted to yell out 'Lower!' I was desperate to feel the sweeping movement of the brush between my legs, but I simply couldn't speak in the face of his amazing self restraint.

My elbows shook and my stomach flinched as the steady motion of the brush worked ever downwards. I wanted to touch him. I wanted to see that powerful chest without the ill-matched shirt and tie. I was desperate to taste him, lick his neck, and consume his cock in my mouth. My tense arms ached more than ever as he finally, blessedly, flicked the damp tip of the paintbrush across my swollen nub, and I screamed out with an overwhelming relief.

Max untied me with uncharacteristic speed, his self-control finally spent, and I yanked off his clothes with an urgency I'd hitherto never experienced. No sooner had my eyes taken in the magnificent dick that was before me, than I enveloped it in my starving mouth. I relished the feel of each pulsating vein against my probing tongue as the first droplets of salty liquid seeped down my throat, and was rewarded by Max's low pitched moans turning to louder and louder grunts.

Pushing me away in a fit of frustration, I found my mouth only briefly bereft as Max's lips touched my own, and his dick slid between my already parted legs. He lifted me up, and slammed me against the wall. I wrapped my legs around his waist, responding to every thrust with one of my own. We both came together, our gasps of mutual satisfaction bouncing around the walls of the studio, before we sagged into a heap onto the partially cleaned wooden floor.

As soon as I regained my breath, I ran across to the discarded paintbrush. It was time I did some art work of my own.

I have a new job now. I occasionally miss sorting out the paintbrushes and watering the flowers, but at least I get to see them regularly as I sit, for as long as required, whilst Max paints his latest muse. Sometimes, he even uses the brushes on the canvas.

Chapter Five

After following up on a recommendation by a friend, I met the sweet shop assistant in the smaller of Kew Garden's coffee houses. She delighted in telling me her story, and I wrote down her account literally word for word as she spoke.

Some fetishes are just bizarre…

Sweets

'Perhaps I should explain that we work in a sweet shop. We sell the old fashioned kind of sweets in jars; Lemon Sherbets, Kola-Kubes, Cherry Lips, Dolly Mixtures, alongside all the new stuff and posh boxes of chocolates.

It all happened quite quickly I guess. It was obvious from the moment I took the job that we wanted each other, but initially we held back. Work isn't the best place after all, especially if there are only two members of staff. Anyway, as I said, it was sort of inevitable really.

So last Thursday evening, there I was, starkers on the bed, watching my boss who was naked, commanding, and utterly gorgeous.

I was not tied to the bed, but I wish I had been. He'd ordered me to stay still, but it was unbelievably difficult to obey as my body desperately wanted to move towards him.

My arms were folded with my hands sat beneath my head, and my legs were pushed up so that my knees pointed into the air. It was as if I was about to undergo some unpleasant medical intrusion.

He'd placed a soft silk cushion under my arse to give him, as he put it, "better visual."

He flashed a little bag in front of my eyes, but made sure I couldn't actually see what it contained. I frowned at his long delicate fingers, unsure of what was coming next. He just smiled.

I tried to concentrate on what he was holding, but the heat surging through my breasts from the whipping they had just received was taking most of my attention. My nipples burnt and longed for a cooling tongue to kiss them better. I had to push my head back harder into my hands to prevent myself from moving them and rubbing myself off.

At last he showed me the packet. It was a Dib-Dab; a packet of loose sherbet with a cherry flavoured lolly conveniently included. When I was a kid I loved to suck all the sherbet off the sticky lolly.

I flinched as he ripped it open. There was something about the way he was looking at me that confirmed that the agony he'd previously inflicted was simply the first course, and that seconds was coming up. I longed to scream out 'Just get on with it!', but the ball gag which he'd lodged in my mouth prevented the luxury of speech, so I just had to content myself with biting down hard onto the black rubber intrusion.

My thighs felt slick with my own juices. I tried hard not to think about the picture I must have presented. As I've said, I wasn't bound, but I was gagged, and my breasts were pressed through a tight black harness, pushing them up and exposing them as an easy target for the short riding crop I had discovered he kept in the corner of his bedroom.

He pulled the lolly out of the packet and put it in his mouth. As he sucked I could feel my nipples tremble. That was what they needed. I felt unbelievably jealous of a bloody sweet!

After what felt like an eternity, he pulled the damp lolly from between his lips and advanced towards me. There was no hanging about. He stuffed its red oval head into me and pushed it until all but the very end of the stick had been swallowed up into my starving hole.

The width of the lolly felt amazing as it stretched me open. I could feel the air rushing in around the thin stick, making me feel empty but full at the same time. I began to shudder in response to the contradiction of sensations, but he slapped my breasts hard and I cried out into my rubber guardian.

'You will not come yet.' His voice was like gravel, and for a second I had to remind myself that I had wanted this too. He began to slide the lollypop up and down and I closed my eyes, trying for all I was worth not to climax. A task made even harder when he knelt and began to lick the mixture of pussy juice and sweet syrup from around my hole.

I was shaking, I couldn't help it. It wasn't going to take much to push me over the edge, even though it had been forbidden. Then he did it. He climbed astride me and sprinkled the sherbet from the Dib-Dab packet all over my tits. The cold sweet dust tickled as it landed on my sweating skin. My hips twitched as I began to fight a losing battle with myself. As his mouth enclosed my right tit, licking up the sherbet, I groaned into silence as the sweet fizzed against his tongue and my chest. By the time he began to feast on my left side I was shaking and bucking so hard I'm surprised he wasn't knocked off.

He took very little notice of the fact that I had disobeyed him until every single drop of the tingling dust had been consumed. Only then did his face become a picture of disgust and lust in glorious combination. I began to shiver, no longer with desire, but in response to the look in his eyes. He picked up a liquorice boot lace from the pile of supplies he'd lifted from the shop. Licking the end to dampen it a little, he lashed my right nipple hard. Tears instantly sprang to my eyes as he stung me again and again.

Then, taking a handful of the laces, he began to coil them around my harnessed breasts. The black strings were cool against my hot flesh and felt heavy against my need to be sucked, caressed and kissed. The ever growing pyramids of sweets created a sticky barrier against the attention I craved. Soon only my two swollen nipples were visible, poking out from the liquorice cones.

My boss stepped back, pleased with his work. After brief consideration he came to my face and finally, mercifully, undid the ball gag. My jaw cracked as he eased the rubber out of my mouth. I longed to thank him, but I was so stiff the words just wouldn't come out. Even if they could've, they didn't really have time to form, as I quickly found his rock hard dick teasing my pleading face.

I licked the end, relishing the wet tip across my dry mouth. He withdrew almost instantly and unwrapped a giant sucking lolly, which he pushed into my mouth saying, 'Work on that girl,' before I even had time to protest.

I was very conscious of how heavy my head felt against my hands. I was rigid from lack of movement and the need in me had already risen to where it had been before my lapse in concentration. It seemed I would have to wait longer still for any allowable relief though, as he obviously had other ideas, and was determined to turn me into some kind of female Bertie Bassett.

He placed a large round dolly mixture on each nipple, effectively making my whole chest into one giant sweet. Then, returning to his collection of stock, he picked up two large liquorice wheels, and placed them over my eyes. The smell of liquorice was becoming quite overpowering and sickly, and I felt disorientated as the room was blocked from my view. Now only the tiny chinks of light which slithered through the cracks in the wheels gave me any sense of time and place.

It was very quiet, except for the occasional slurp my tongue made against the lolly as I attempted to suck it smaller and prevent myself from gagging on its huge presence.

I have no idea how long I'd laid there in my liquorice uniform. I was aware of the occasional flash of light; perhaps he was opening and closing the curtains or was unable to decide whether to have the light on or off. When, at last, he touched me my skin leapt and even the lollipop could not stifle my sigh of relief.

Slowly, painfully slowly, he began to unravel the liquorice strings from around my tits. They made small popping noises as he pulled them away from my tacky skin. I could imagine the brown smudges of colouring that would remain in their absence.

Underneath my sweetie mask I could just detect shifts in his movements as he gathered up the laces. The allsorts had long since fallen off my red tips and my breasts felt even more vulnerable than before, something not helped by the continuing presence of the restraining harness. I stiffened at the thought that he might whip my tits again. I needn't have worried though. He had other plans.

He lifted each half of my mask off with his teeth, grazing my eye brows slightly. I blinked in the light and focused on his hands, which were still holding the retrieved laces. He laid them carefully, in a regimented row across my stomach. Then, taking one at a time, he snaked them down my skin, which seemed to singe at the touch. As he trailed them closer and closer to my pussy I began to panic. Automatically I sat up, bringing my crushed hands round to my stomach, catching his neatly arranged rows of liquorice as they fell.

The flash of anger that crossed his face made me instantly regret losing my concentration, but then suddenly he smiled. It was a heart melting smile which reminded me in an instant what I was doing there. 'Okay, I guess you've been a good girl - you can watch.'

He took the liquorice off me and helped me up to the old arm chair in the corner of the room. As my back was pushed against the seat, he dragged a small coffee table away from the wall and rested my feet on it, spreading my legs as wide as they would go.

'I obviously can't trust you not to interfere, so I'm going to have to tie your hands together.' He seemed more amused than cross, as if he'd already achieved his aim and now he could relax. Perhaps he'd come already? I wasn't sure, but how else could he maintain his composure for so long without shooting his load?

He dragged his belt out of his discarded jeans and pulled the buckle clasp tight around my wrists, resting my hands across my lap. I watched as he began to tease my feet with a long string of liquorice. I felt goose pimples spring up all over me at the amazing sensations shooting up my legs. I wouldn't have thought it possible for him to move so slowly. He inched the lace around my feet, taking an agonising eternity to reach my knees. As it slithered upwards it reminded me of a snake; hungry, searching for a dark hole in which to devour its prey.

That's when I realised what he was going to do. I couldn't help but squirm. My clit was on fire, and I swear if he had simply touched my tits I would've come there and then. 'Oh no you don't,' he pushed the flat of one hand against me, pinning me to the chair whilst continuing the liquorice's slow dance upwards.

My skin jumped as it finally reached the tender soaked skin at the top of my legs. That was when I saw him take a deep breath. It was the first sign I had seen of his own need demanding some more immediate attention. His pace quickened. 'Stay still.' He spoke roughly as he placed the narrow end of the liquorice lace between my pussy lips, and began to push and thread its entire length into my desperate body. I couldn't help but protest as the string twisted itself up inside me, its movements now unpredictable. Once its complete length had been engulfed, he started again with another lace.

My tears came properly then, I simply couldn't help it. They silently streamed down my liquorice smudged face. I'd been kept on the brink for so long.

Again he stuffed the last inch of sweet into me, making sure he avoided any contact with my red hot clit.

'Not long now sweetie.' His voice was gentle, so contrary to the evening that had past. I wanted to reach out to him, hold him, but my tethered hands forbade any such expressions of affection.

He stood back and took a drink of water. 'I don't think I have ever seen anything so delicious.' He knelt down and pulled the table from beneath my feet, lifting my legs up onto his shoulders. 'You have no idea,' he spoke softly. 'How difficult it has been to wait.' I looked into his eyes as he continued, 'I don't think I have ever felt so hungry.'

He began to eat then, whilst I spasmed in relief against his greedy face. When he eventually stood up, black liquorice stains ran from his mouth, which he then smeared against my own, before finally filling me with something far more satisfying than sweets.

It was about a month later when my boss finally plucked up enough courage to show me the photographs he had taken. I couldn't believe they were of me. You should see the hard on he gets every time he looks at them. Boy does that man like liquorice.'

CHAPTER SIX

Many of the stories I have collected have caused me to pause for thought. I frequently wonder how people come to do what they do. Why they enjoy what they enjoy. Now and again a story inspires me to try things out myself. 'Sweets' is one such story. I hope you will forgive the self-indulgence, but I was beyond curious.

The Experiment

It was the idea of the sherbet on my tits that I couldn't shake, and it got me thinking that there must be other areas of the anatomy where such confectionary could be utilised to an erotic effect.

I began to think back to the sweets of my youth. Rhubarb and Custard, Mint Humbugs, proper Marathon bars, or Snickers as they are now known. Then it hit me. Moon Dust or maybe Popping Candy. I knew what I wanted to do with that straight away.

It took some time to track down the Moon Dust, but once I had my purchase I arranged for a fully appraised friend to call and help with my research. He wasted no time in setting up the camera, all the better for me to gauge reactions, expressions, responses and so on. Then he stripped, as I did, in a rather business-like way.

A little cold perhaps? Yet this is how it is in science. After all this was just an experiment; just one of many my friend and I have privately conducted over the years.

He likes to be told what to do. He likes to be teased by being told what will happen to him, and then the frustration of being made to wait. So I oblige him, and make him wait.

By the time I am ready to carry out the purpose of this exercise he is very erect, very ready, as am I.

I shall uncharacteristically skip the details of our warm up. Let's just say that I have already had to smack him for begging me to hurry, but now I needed some results too. I positioned him to my best advantage, and to that of the camcorder.

He sits on the edge of my bed, his legs wide, his cock at mouth level, as I sit on my knees before him. We regard each other carefully as I rip open the wrapper.

I dip my finger into the packet and immediately feel it pop and crackle against my skin. I scoop out a little and rub it just inside his mouth, telling him what I was about to do with the rest of the packet at the same time. He squirms and shuffles, imagining what it might be like.

I've made him yell out before, groan, moan, mewl and many other associated noises, but until now I had never made him scream. His reaction was incredible as the tiny particles of dust exploded against his penis.

I felt good too. It was as if his already large cock was bigger than ever before, expanding with the dust I was sucking off him.

I pulled back and quickly sat astride him, and screamed myself as the sweetness which had stuck to him now exploded inside me.

We declared the experiment a success. In fact it wasn't long before I placed a bulk order for a delivery of Moon Dust with that particular sweet company.

Oh yes, it's fucking fantastic on tits as well!!

CHAPTER SEVEN

I'm not sure if I would have believed the next story if I hadn't met the woman involved. I came across her via an advert she'd placed at the back of a car magazine, offering her, very specific, personal services. I quickly phoned the high rate number and, having explained my interest, arranged to meet her on my next trip to London. Trust me; she is every motor fanatic's dream shag.

Car Love

Even though the gag was securely tied, muffled groans escaped from the corners of her mouth. Dressed only in high heels that matched the burgundy of the car before her, she awaited instructions.

The garage was cool and dark but for the yellow beams provided by the sports car's headlights, whose engine purred seductively.

He steered her forwards across the hood, so that her legs were pushed hard against the private number plate. Her breasts, still recovering from seemingly endless teasing with a silk handkerchief, quivered as the cold of the room was replaced with heat as they were crushed against the vibrating bonnet.

She was still shuffling her heels to find a comfortable position when the first blow struck her exposed rump. Biting down onto the paisley scarf tied between her damp lips, she concentrated on riding out the exquisite pain. He struck again. The leather belt striped her burning arse so it formed a neat criss-cross pattern on her tanned flesh.

Arms outstretched, hugging the throbbing metal, the need which he'd spent the last hour engineering in her finally became unbearable.

He paused behind her, admiring the view for a split second, before he too could no longer wait. Grasping her hips, he buried himself into her, pumping in time to the engine ticking-over beneath them. His black cock was so tight that it provided a delicious pain of its own. She pressed her clit onto the unyielding metal, letting the spasms course through her body.

He removed the gag and watched as, unbidden, his expensive slave knelt to lick the faultless bodywork clean of their juices.

This woman loved her car.

CHAPTER EIGHT

I met her quite by chance as she sat next to me on the tube from Richmond to London Waterloo. She was on her way to do some serious shopping. Her eagerness to chat was obvious from the moment I laid eyes on her. After some initial small talk, I confessed my professional interest, and asked if she'd mind expanding on the story she'd just told me.

My request that she tell her tale into my Dictaphone met some resistance, but eventually, after quite a lot of persuasion and promises of anonymity, she agreed to let me record her experience over a coffee and slice of cake at the very back of the oriental coffee shop at Waterloo Station.

Late Developer

'It would be unfair to say I hate my job, but it has been so hectic lately that the prospect of a little pampering was more than welcome. I was nervous though, I'd never been to a beauty salon before. My first boyfriend had once described me as "unbelievably natural." No make up, legs shaved not waxed, hair combed if it was lucky, and clothes that were cheap, but most of all, comfortable. I was never sure if he was paying me a compliment or complaining.

Anyway. I had been having a tough time at work and my friend, June, had decided that I needed a treat, so there I was unexpectedly having my virgin face covered in make up.

It felt very strange having all that powder and eye liner and stuff on, but not quite as odd as I had imagined it might be. June sat in the room with me as the beautician, who couldn't have been more than 18, tutted in disbelief that a woman of 36 couldn't apply mascara without looking like something from a bad 1960s horror movie.

As I sat there having myself "done" I tried to imagine what I must look like, having been barred from looking in a mirror until it was all over. All the way through, June uttered encouraging comments, and we laughed and giggled like a couple of kids.

Finally, after what seemed like weeks, I was declared finished and a mirror was magically produced.

It wasn't me. It just wasn't. The eyes were bigger, more defined. The skin was darker with a subtle glow. The eye lashes were long and each one stood out. The lips shone bronze in the harsh light of the tiny white room. June was smiling broadly. 'Well?' she asked.

I honestly didn't know what I thought. I said 'I can't believe it, I look so different. It's great, but it's going to take some getting used to.'

'I think you look amazing.' June was so definite. I think I must have looked mildly offended as she quickly added, 'Not that you didn't before.'

I wasn't convinced, but I suppose my eyes did look pretty good, even if I did feel like I was looking back at the reflection of a completely different person.

The beautician packed up her things and we left. June was chatting away and we decided that we were having too much fun to go our separate ways, so we hit the off licence and brought some white wine before heading to her flat and dialling for a pizza. Whilst we waited for the food to arrive we hunted for a DVD to veg out in front of.

It was like being 18; or what I imagine being 18 should feel like. I ignored my teenage years really, reading novels whilst others partied and had fun – I am definitely a late developer.

The film was good; light and rather silly. With hindsight I suppose that June had been slightly subdued during the film. She certainly hadn't laughed as much as me. I just assumed I'd had more wine than she had.

June hadn't lived in her flat long, so I politely agreed when she said she'd give me a tour round. It was much bigger than I'd expected and I did the usual "oohing" and "ahhing" at the décor, some of which was even genuine.

When we reached her bedroom I found myself pulled to the window. The view was stunning. It was an almost stereotypical scene of the English countryside. There was a river, a wood in the distance, and the comforting sound of the world getting on without us. It was quite breathtaking.

It must have been a few minutes before I realised that June had moved closer to me. Her fingertips brushing, seemingly accidentally, against mine. I looked at her and smiled.

Obviously you can guess the rest. I think I'm still in shock to be honest. It is as if everything's changed. Changed for the better. How could I not have known? Not seen?'

It took a bit of persuading to get the rest of this tale – it certainly isn't the most explosive or shocking story I've ever collected, but it is sweet and genuine, and the smirk that developed as my coffee companion eventually spoke made my persuasive efforts well worth while.

'It was quite a light evening. Our fingers touched again, and it was like the fabled electric shock. I'm not sure what actually gave me the confidence to wrap my hand completely around hers. It felt good, and for quite a long time we just looked out of the window together.

I think I moved first, I'm really not sure. For a while it all seemed to happen in slow motion, like it does on TV when you're not sure if the screen couple are going to kiss. Well, once our lips did meet, life definitely speeded up again.

Her mouth was so incredibly soft. I closed my eyes. I daren't look at her in case it broke the spell. The kiss both lasted for ages and no time at all. Then I felt her hands stroking my back, my neck and, oh so wonderful, my chest.

I thought I'd explode. I have never felt so turned on simply by someone's fingers caressing me through cotton. I couldn't just stand there. I yanked at my tucked-in top and pulled it swiftly over my head. It was only then, with my arms and bra exposed, that I dared glance at June's face. The fear was gone. I didn't care that I had known her for years, or that I had never wanted a woman before. Suddenly it was the most natural thing in the world.

Her hands traced the edges of my pale cream bra. I remember a voice at the back of my head saying thank goodness I'd put my best one on. The rest of me was very much mixed up in the incredible sensations her fingertips were creating. I could feel my tits swelling beneath the flimsy material, which now seemed far too tight.

No one spoke though. Maybe we weren't ready to actually give a name to the mind-blowing thing that was happening.

I couldn't suppress a sigh as her gentle movements suddenly became harder. Her palms crushed against my breasts, kneading them like dough, until at last, blessedly, she pulled each breast out of my bra so that they nestled above it. June murmured something appreciative that I didn't quite catch. I was too busy groaning with relief as her soft mouth settled over one nipple and her probing fingers sharply pinched the other. The gentleness of the one caress, and the violence of the other, was overwhelming. I came quicker than I ever have in my whole life.

June continued her ministrations as I stood there shaking. She only paused in her attentions to swap her lips and fingers from one side to the other. The heat of my abused nipple was quickly stifled by her lips, prolonging my orgasm until I could barely hold myself up. I grabbed her to steady myself, and in the process we both fell back on to the bed.

I'm honestly not sure what order things happened in next. With hindsight I can't believe I just went with it. I didn't need to think about what to do. It came so naturally. I'm still so amazed by the wonderfulness of it all. The texture of her mouth, the smell of her skin, and the exquisite feel and taste of her clit. Her full, heavy chest, and the sharp intake of her breath as I tongued her, plunging June into the first orgasm I had ever given a woman.

I can't quite take it all in.

My friend June!

I'm seeing her later; that's why I'm here in town. I'm off to buy some new knickers. Something special…'

CHAPTER NINE

I've known this young man via a mutual friend for a while now, and I must confess that I had always been a little curious about him. When an opportunity arose to get to know him a little better, I grasped it willingly. It had been way too long since my last man, and anyway, I take my collecting very seriously.

Treasure

'Nice rocking chair.'

'Thanks. It was a birthday present.' I watched as he explored the contents of my bedroom; the drawers under the bed, the clutter on the window sills; everywhere.

From my rocking chair I watched as his slightly dated, almost foppish hair, fell over his eyes as he lent down to a large battered trunk at the foot of my bed. He was like a little boy searching for treasure.

'What's in here?'

I didn't reply, just gestured for him to open it and find out. I wish I'd had a camera to capture the wide-eyed expression on his face as he creaked back the heavy lid. 'Is this stuff all yours?'

I couldn't decide if he was freaked out by his discovery or amazed that the nice girl he'd just spent several hours sat next to at a mutual friends' dinner party had a large assortment of sex toys within easy reach of her bed.

'Yes. All mine.' He plunged both hands into the trunk and rummaged about. After a minute or two of happy hunting he pulled out a nicely weighted black paddle: leather coated with a short handle.

'My favourite weapon of choice,' he declared, 'simple but extremely effective, don't you agree?'

My heart began to beat a little faster. I had come to the decision early on in the evening that I was going to have sex with this man. Only now did I see it was going to be even more fun than I had previously thought.

'I have another favourite actually.' He raised his eyebrows at me questioningly. 'Maybe I'll show you later, if you like? If you're good.'

'I'm intrigued,' he smiled as he pulled an assortment of toys from the box. Masks, chains, chuffs, whips, dildos and more. 'I seem to have walked into a fetishist's heaven?' He made the statement a question. I ignored it, smiled and continued to rock back and forth in my chair, watching him behave like a child in a sweet shop.

'Would you like a drink?' I reverted to hostess. I didn't want him to reach the toy hidden at the very bottom of the box. That was for later. I knew I had to use it on him, and it would be even better if it was a total surprise

'Please. It was a nice dinner party, but not nearly enough alcohol.'

'I agree. Red or white?'

As I poured out the red wine he'd requested, I acknowledged to myself that once again this would be a one off thing. Sad really, I could like this guy, but sex was already out there. It was too late. Once I had allowed him to discover my treasure there had been no going back. 'Fine; so let's make the most of it,' I muttered to myself as I drank some of my wine before topping up my glass and carrying them both out of the kitchen.

I found him in the living room sifting through my DVD collection. Frankly I would have been more impressed if I'd caught him looking at the vast collection of books which lined the walls, but you can't have everything. I passed him his drink.

'Good collection.' He had obviously expected wall to wall romance, with perhaps the odd comedy thrown in, not a catalogue of sex and violence. After his earlier discovery perhaps he shouldn't have been so surprised.

'Hey, you've got porn. How cool are you?!' he beamed. This guy might have reached the age of 28, but he was obviously clinging onto teenage-hood as hard as he could. He was acting as if he'd just found an old and much loved copy of *Mayfair* under his bed. 'I've never met a girl who had porn DVDs before.'

'Of course you have.' I took his glass back off him and placed it next to mine on the fire place. 'You just haven't met one who has them on display before.'

'Perhaps.' I had shifted the mood on an hour, and to his credit he didn't question my decision.

'Tell me,' I asked as I took his hand, 'that paddle you were admiring earlier, did you imagine yourself giving or receiving?'

He regarded me closely, as if he was making a tough decision. 'Actually I enjoy both. But at that particular moment, judging by the rest of the gear you have stashed away, I wondered what it would be like to be under your control.'

As he spoke he lowered his bright blue eyes meekly and hung his arms loosely at his sides. He had obviously played this game before. I swallowed down my delight, and studied his subservient posture for a minute. My mind was full of possibilities; but I knew exactly where to start.

'I think we should lose that t-shirt.' He didn't move so I adopted a sterner voice. 'Take it off.'

'Please, Miss.' He avoided looking at my face; concentrating on my bare feet instead.

'What is it boy?' I gave up being nice; he obviously didn't want me to be. Just as well really, considering what I ultimately had in mind.

'Make me. Please, make me.'

I hadn't been able to disguise my smile as delicious sparks of lust shot down my spine. I allowed myself a split second of weakness before I reclaimed my dominant position and barked, 'Take it off you lazy bitch.'

His cheeks flushed as my orders cut into the otherwise silent room. He tugged the white cotton over his head in one swift movement. Keeping his eyes cast down, he shuffled a little closer.

'That's better'. I took his hand and led him to the bedroom, where I stood him in front of the treasure box. 'Such disobedience is not permitted in this house,' I opened the trunk. 'I think some punishment is due.' I held his chin firmly between my fingers and lifted his head so he could look into my eyes. 'What do you think, bitch?'

'Yes ma'am. I should be punished ma'am.' He looked down again. This boy could act. I felt my body responding to the tension which sizzled between us. He was waiting to see what I'd pull from the box. I knew what I wanted to do; but not yet. This situation was too good to rush.

'I'd like you to sit in the rocking chair and shut your eyes until I tell you what to do next.' He went. He sat. He closed his eyes.

I pushed the heavy trunk away from the end of the bed so that I could walk all the way around it. Then, glancing at him to ensure his eyes were shut, I took out a selection of instruments I might need, and a few more I would not. I wasn't entirely sure exactly what I'd use, but I knew what effect seeing a pile of whips, masks and nipple clamps would have when he saw them heaped on the bed.

I hid my end game toy under the duvet and shut the trunk's hard lid. Then I took off all my clothes and slipped on my much loved PVC bodice; pulling the laces tight so that my breasts stuck provocatively over the top. Then I eased on my long shiny black boots. I could feel the power surging through me as I donned my mistress attire. I didn't bother with knickers; they'd only get in the way.

When I was ready I separated out a long belt that I kept with my other treasures, and slid it under the trunk so that an end stuck out either side of the its width. I picked up a whip. I might have looked like a stereotypical dominatrix from the front of a porn mag, but I felt incredible as I regarded my intended victim. He had no idea what was coming next, and that knowledge alone caused my already turned on body to ache for some attention of its own. I took a gulp of air and ignored my rising need. It was time to have some fun.

'Open your eyes and come here.'

He stood, and I was gratified to see that my outfit had the desired effect. His already stiff dick visibly swelled beneath his jeans. I pointed at his bulge with the whip 'I think we'd better lose those trousers.' This time he obeyed instantly 'and the boxers.' His white pants hit the deck so fast that I had to stifle a grin. He was gorgeous. Not too toned. No horrible over-worked six-pack, just a dick which I had to force myself not to kneel in front of straight away. Tasting how luscious he was, was going to have to wait.

'Good boy.' I trailed the whip down his chest and felt him quiver beneath its touch, before throwing it onto the bed. 'Now, as you can see I have extracted a few items from my box of treasure.'

He flicked his eyes towards the pile of toys. His face paled but he didn't flinch and he didn't ask questions.

I picked up a long pink ribbon and tickled his balls with its slightly frayed end. Then, ignoring his sharp intake of breath, I wrapped one end around them, knotting the fabric loosely, so that it would tighten slightly if I pulled the other end, which I held like a long lead. I gave the ribbon a gentle experimental tug. He gasped as his eyes stared at what I had done to him. He looked beautiful. Pretty in pink.

I pointed to the trunk. I knew he understood, but he wanted telling. 'On your knees. Now.' He knelt before me, his face tantalizingly near my pussy. I have no idea how I resisted ordering him to start licking. Instead I told him to lie across the trunk.

His head and neck hung down, causing his hair to brush the carpet. He had to support himself by placing his lower arms on the floor. His legs crouched down at the foot of the trunk, exposing his back and buttocks to whatever whim I chose, the long ribbon hanging between his parted legs. I gave him just enough time to realise how uncomfortable he was before I took the ends of the leather belt and drew them together, buckling him tightly to the trunk.

His shocked gasp as he found himself pinioned was wonderful. I guess he'd been expecting cuffs or chains, not a thick leather belt across the small of his back. Now I really did wish I had a camera handy. He looked fantastic. I ran a single finger along the edges of the belt, tickling his smooth trapped skin. I listened with satisfaction as he sighed under my touch.

I grabbed the ribbon lead and began to trail it across his arse. First over one cheek, then the other, before very slowly slipping it up and down his crack. I tugged it slightly with each movement, increasing the pressure on his squashed balls. His arse puckered like a hungry mouth; he was already opening for me. Excellent.

I dropped the ribbon and went around to his face. Picking up a long cane, I held it under his chin, forcing him to look up at me. The blood had run to his head, but his arms were still holding him. He must have been stronger than he looked. 'This,' I said, flexing the cane between my fingers, 'is my favourite method of correction.'

His eyes pleaded with me, but I wasn't sure if he was willing me to hurry up and hit him, or if he wanted me to show some mercy. 'I know you prefer the paddle, so, in the interests of fairness, I have got that handy too.' This time he visibly winced.

I knelt and kissed his beautifully flushed face, before returning to his backside. I smoothed the end of the cane against his arse, and then flicked it at him lightly, listening to the neat cracking noise it made.

That was enough preparation. Besides, if I'd had to wait much longer I would have run the risk of losing control. I raised the cane and whacked it down onto his right buttock. He yelled into the carpet. I followed it with another smack, and another, and soon I was wishing that I'd pulled a gag out of the trunk before I'd tied him to it.

The collection of stripe marks against his flesh grew as his howls increased in volume. Finally he cried out. 'Please!' But he didn't ask me to stop.

I dropped the cane and took up the paddle, bringing it down hard across his hot red arse. He yelped, but his cries had lost their agonised edge. He had reached cross-over. Any minute now he'd be begging me to release him so he could thrust himself into my collected but quietly desperate body.

I continued to administer his beating with one hand, and began to finger myself with the other.

After a while, I abandoned the paddle, and was rewarded by his groan of loss as the pain stopped. I knelt down and traced a sticky finger over his dark rim. It rippled beneath my touch as I pushed a digit just inside the grasping lips.

'Oh God!' His grunted shout was my signal to pull my hidden strap-on from beneath the duvet and clip it into its vinyl belt. He was trying to rub himself off against the trunk, but I knew my business and the belt held him firm. He'd get no relief that way.

I stroked my fake penis between my legs, lubricating it with my own juices, before clicking it onto the belt. If he had any doubts about what I was about to do, I dismissed them by pressing myself against his arse, cramming the plastic cock between his yielding cheeks.

He groaned deeply, and I could see sweat start to prickle across his back. Pushing down harder, I was soon engulfed and imagined how his trapped stomach would be contracting as he struggled between pleasure, pain and holding onto the contents of his bowels.

I relished in the feeling of power as I lay on top of his back and began to set the pace, ramming in and out of him as slowly as I could bear. With each movement I scraped the edge of the leather belt against my clit. Bliss.

As his growls turned to moans he cried out. 'I can't hold on. Fuck me harder!' I did as I was told and began to thrust in and out of him as fast as I could, whilst yanking the ribbon hard so that it dug into his trapped balls. My bodice stuck to his back as our combined perspiration sucked us even closer together. I could feel the build up of my own climax wash over me as he roared into the carpet.

I eased out, enjoying the slurping sound his arse made as it contracted with loss. I threw off my dick and undid the belt. His arms were shaking as I pulled him to his feet, releasing his swollen balls from the damp ribbon. I admired his dripping cock, which was still covered in the creamy spunk he'd shot all over my trunk.

He looked at me with undisguised greed; all submission gone. He tugged open the laces of my bustier and freed the under-sides of my breasts. As he attacked my tits with his mouth I realised I had been quite wrong. This was not the only experience of his company I was going to have. Picking up two ropes, he pushed me into my rocking chair, and licked me to a second shuddering climax.

As he tied my arms to the chair's arm rests, I wondered how many stories I was going to get out of my new acquaintance before we had worked our way through the entire contents of my treasure box.

CHAPTER TEN

Top shelf magazines are always worth a read. Not the stories or the photographs necessarily, but the editorials and the names of the staff that put them together. Outside the exaggerated imaginings of their monthly publications, they often have their own research to do. Many of these journalists' experiences are exactly the sort of thing I look for.

Karen had worked for *Erotique Magazine* for twelve months. From standard brothels to punishment dens, from S&M clubs to fantasist's alien sex parties, she'd seen and reported from them all. So when Karen's editor asked her to write an article about a new venture he'd come across, she agreed without hesitation.

Executive School

Fastening the tops of her stockings, Karen took some deep breaths. She was gearing herself up to be a professional reporter, and not just a voyeuristic onlooker. It was no good entering into these situations, only to be overtaken by personal lust. Although Karen had begun to wonder if perhaps she hadn't become rather too good at putting her own needs to the back of her mind. Recently she'd noticed that she could watch a woman being licked out by a probing tongue, or a man being whipped until he screamed and shot his load from his body, without so much as a hardened nipple.

Her last two boyfriends had both commented on this hardness of heart, her pleasure being almost impossible to bring off. Karen knew her reaction to pornography and the act of sex in general had changed, becoming almost mundane. Still, she loved her job. It was worth it. Most of the time.

Karen checked her watch, almost 10pm. The class was due to start at 10.30. She should leave. Hoisting her long auburn hair into a pony tail, she examined her appearance in the hall mirror. Not too business-like; she'd rejected her suit jacket in favour of a soft lilac cashmere sweater, but held onto the suit trousers and medium heels for the required professional gloss.

As Karen settled into the back of the cab she'd hailed, she produced the evening's brief out of her shoulder bag. *"The Executive School. A safe and friendly environment to expand those lost skills of fulfilment."* That was all the flyer said. Her editor, Charles, hadn't been able to expand that much. He'd just heard that the education dished out was based on sexual fulfilment and that, as their readers were always in pursuit of new techniques, it would be worth a look. He'd arranged it all he said, and they were expecting her.

Her mobile phone buzzed in her bag.

'Karen?'

'I'm just on my way Charles, don't worry.'

'I thought I'd better come clean before you got there.' Charles sounded slightly uncomfortable as he spoke.

Karen was immediately suspicious. 'What do you mean? Come clean about what?'

'You aren't going along to report, well not just to report. You're going in undercover. As far as the class are concerned, you're one of them.'

'WHAT?!' Karen shouted down her phone, causing the cab driver to look around in concern.

Charles elaborated. 'You are to join in and write about the experience afterwards.'

'Join in?' Karen spoke slowly, not quite believing what she was hearing. 'Exactly what am I joining in?'

'Look honey, this job gets to people. I should know, I've been doing it along time. Too much exposure and not enough action, it's bad for you to forget what it's like to feel. You can become desensitised if you're not careful.'

Karen could almost hear her last boyfriend's words as her editor spoke.

'Charles, I really don't want...'

'You'll love it.'

'But I can't! Watching, being apart from it is one thing, but honestly,' Karen dropped her voice to a whisper. 'What if they want me to take my clothes off?'

'Lucky them.'

'Charles!'

'Karen. This has cost the company big,' Charles put his chief editor's voice back on. Do not waste our money. I want a full, in-depth, personalised report written tomorrow morning.'

'But...'

'The man you report to is called Mark. He thinks you are a bored divorced career woman who wants a bit of pep to her life.'

'How dare...'

'AND,' Charles raised his voice to stem her flood of complaints. 'He thinks you are loaded. The fees he charges, you'd have to be. Call me the second it's over.' He hung up.

Sweat prickled across Karen's palms. She was a reporter, not a participant. No one ever gave Kate Adie a gun and told her to go shoot someone to see how it felt for God's sake. She read the flyer again. It still said nothing.

The taxi pulled up outside the hotel where the class was to be held. Karen paid the driver with shaking hands and stood, uncertain, on the pavement. She could run, but she really didn't want Charles to sack her. Maybe she should blow her cover and ask to be a casual observer. Or perhaps, a small voice nagged at her from the back of her mind: '*You might enjoy yourself. It might help you to remember the point of all this stuff you write. The magazine was designed to turn people on for heaven's sake; why not you?*'

Taking another calming breath, she marched into the foyer, headed to Reception, and asked for the Fountain Suite. Karen chanted silently under her breath, 'I'm a reporter. I'm a professional. I can be involved without being truly involved, I CAN do this.' She pushed her shoulders back, stood up straight and headed to the door of the suite.

Her tentative knock caused the door to be opened by a young woman, beyond which stood a well built middle-aged man. Mark, she presumed. He was accompanied by two men and one other woman. Instant partners. Karen's stomach contracted with nerves, she felt like a high class hooker on her first hit.

'Welcome, welcome. You must be Karen.' Mark's infusive greeting made her feel more, rather than less, scared, as the door attendant ushered her over to the others. They had "money" written all over them. Designer clothes, designer jewellery, good shoes, yet they also had that "alone after thirty" quality about them. 'So,' Karen thought to herself, '*This is a class of people who've been business professionals for so long that they've forgotten how to let go. And I'm one of them. Shit.*'

Whilst coats were taken and hung up, and introductions made and forgotten, Karen looked about her. Comfortable sofas lined the walls of the warm subtly lit room, a huge double bed sat knowingly in the corner of the room, and cushions covered the luxury carpeted floor.

'Ladies and gentlemen,' Mark spoke softly but with command. 'I would like to thank you for coming here tonight, and for your continued discretion upon leaving us when the session is complete.' Karen felt his eyes focus on her; did he already know she was detailed to report on all she discovered here?

Mark brushed a lightly greying hair out of his face and continued. 'Reasons of financial success bring you here tonight. You all, according to your personal statements, have no trouble attracting partners, yet you are unable to let yourself go enough to enjoy or provide enjoyment once you and they are, shall we say, *in flagrante delicto.*'

Karen didn't have time to wonder what statement Charles had concocted on her behalf as Mark continued. 'We will begin with mere observation. My assistant Amy,' he gestured to the young lady who had opened the door, 'has kindly agreed to help me with the initial demonstration.'

No more than 23-years-old, petite with shoulder length dyed bright red hair, Amy smiled with the arrogant confidence of someone who knows their body is perfect. Karen, trying and failing to remain professional, hated her already.

Classical music began to play in the background, as Mark invited the students to kick off their shoes and sit on the cushions. Amy walked before them and, on an indication from Mark, began to slowly unbutton her blouse. It wasn't a striptease as such, but it was certainly staged to titillate the viewer. Karen's practiced eye noticed the almost instant swelling within the two pairs of trousers either side of her.

As Amy's flawless stomach appeared from beneath her white blouse, Karen heard the other woman gasp. All were rapt upon the girl, except for her, she watched the watchers. That was when it dawned on her. There was a beautiful woman standing before her in stockings, suspenders, a minimal bra and thong, and she felt nothing. Not a thing. Her mind was too full of how she'd record the spectacle on the pages of her magazine. Could Charles have been right? Had she forgotten how to feel? Had she pushed professional detachment too far?

The next few moments passed without Karen taking in what was happening. She was vaguely aware that Mark was standing next to Amy, showing the group how to caress a girl's breast and receive a more than satisfactory response. Karen was snapped out of her introspection by a mewing sound issuing from Amy's lips. She wanted to believe that it was fake, but the girl's tits were swelling beneath their silk covering, and there was no denying the slight damp patch that was creeping across her satin thong. Tension hung in the room as there, in front of them, Amy came, rocking beneath Mark's gentle but decisive touch.

'Karen, are you with us?' Mark was looking at her. 'You were miles away.'

Karen realised that her female counterpart had her blouse off and the men were looking nervously, but hungrily, at her. Was she supposed to be taking her top off too?

Mark's voice broke through her thoughts. 'Come on, there's little you can learn without practice. Top off, I'm sure you will find this a rewarding experience.'

There seemed little point in protesting, so she pulled off her jumper, revealing her unfussy cream silk bra. Instantly, despite the warmth of the room, goose pimples appeared on her skin.

'In order to heighten the sensations I will blindfold the women. The men will then draw straws for you, not that there is a short straw I hasten to add.' Mark chuckled at his own joke, everyone else was too focused on what was about to happen to make a sound.

Amy approached with two black velvet masks, and before Karen could protest, she found herself slipped into darkness as she sat on the soft cushioned floor wishing she'd been paying attention to what Mark had shown the others. Seconds later, tentative fingers begin to stray across her encased nipples, and rubbed her hidden areoles. She tried hard to concentrate on the feelings themselves and forget about how she was going to write them down.

Karen could hear the woman sat next to her beginning to sigh. Should she be sighing too? The unknown fingers began to brush the tips of Karen's nipples, which responded by tightening beneath the silk. It felt good and she didn't want it to end, but as the woman next to her changed her sighs to cries of 'Oh my God!' and was obviously climbing fast into ecstasy, her own partner gave up and his hands moved away.

She could hear whispers and then Mark's voice saying, 'Slightly more direct action perhaps.' Karen could almost feel the heat of their eyes; she knew they were all looking at her. Her insides squirmed at the thought, she was the one who observed and analysed, not the other way around.

Karen's skin jumped as the cups of her bra were pushed beneath her chest. It felt good to be free of the tight material and even better when a set of fingers returned to her flesh. Karen closed her eyes under her blindfold and focused on the sensations. The slow ignition she needed was just starting to spark her body into life when her partner gave an audible sigh of defeat.

The blindfold was removed and Karen blinked against the light, before taking in the faces before her. She coloured violently and began to babble. 'I'm sorry, it was lovely, it's just I...' She stopped, unable to go on. The man opposite her, presumably her partner, looked crestfallen. 'It wasn't your fault, really, it's me. I'm, well, hard work. Sorry.'

Mark beamed at her. 'Well done. It takes a lot to admit that you have a problem becoming aroused. I think some relaxation exercises would be of benefit to you, and perhaps us all.'

The group were led over towards the king sized bed. 'Amy, if you please.' Mark gestured to the bed. Amy stripped off her remaining clothing, and lay across the bed, face down.

Karen couldn't think what the other members of the group were doing there. As she glanced at them, each obviously turned on and eager for the next event, they didn't seem to need any help at all.

Mark, who seemed to be the only one apart from her that wasn't visibly aroused, began to stroke Amy's backside. He parted her legs a little and began to run a single finger along and around, but not over, her arsehole. 'This is a good area to tease. The frustration of not actually touching the opening will aid your partner's desire.' He moved his hands from her backside, down her legs, then up again to the small of her back, and on towards her shoulders. 'Firm movements, but without the intense grip of a thorough massage. It relaxes both you and your partner and is, in itself, very sexy.'

Amy rose from the bed, her body flushed with barely disguised lust. There was no doubt she was one hot babe.

'Ladies, take your remaining garments off please. If you would prefer not to strip in front of us you may go behind those screens.' Mark pointed to a small sheltered area in the corner of the room. Karen fled there instantly, followed more slowly by her comrade.

'What's your name?' Karen whispered.

'Freya. Yours?'

'Karen. Why are you here? You don't look like you need any help to me. None of you do.'

'I can't speak for the men, but you're right, I don't.' Freya giggled 'But I'm getting a real kick out of this.' She laughed at

Karen's expression. 'I like to look, I like to be watched, and it's a great opportunity to see other women naked.'

Karen was far more shocked than someone of her profession should have been. 'So why not just get a girlfriend?'

'I prefer men, but I like to look at women too.' Freya threw off her knickers with casual confidence. 'You're beautiful by the way.'

Karen froze for a second, feeling even more under scrutiny than she would have done if she'd taken her clothes off in front of the men.

'Come on honey, get those knickers off.'

With an extreme effort Karen yanked them down and followed her comrade beyond the screen, trying not to smile as Freya instantly shed her air of confidence for her audience. Karen didn't dare look at the other faces, but could see that their partners were also naked now, and there was no disguising the fact that they liked what they saw.

Laying face down next to Freya, Karen closed her eyes and tried to slow down her heart-beat by taking a deep lungful of air. She could hear Mark speaking quietly. 'Begin in your own time gentlemen.'

As the soft palms of whichever wealthy office man was smoothing her skin moved up and down her body, Karen felt herself sink into the amazingly soft goose down duvet. Now if she could just stop her mind working overtime she'd get somewhere.

Whilst teasing fingers began to stroke around her firm buttocks, Karen opened her eyes and looked straight into Freya's, who smiled and mouthed, 'Isn't this gorgeous.'

She smiled back at the stunning dark haired woman that lay naked only inches away, and felt the first real stirrings of arousal.

Freya mouthed again, 'I want to kiss you.'

Karen's body twitched and she felt the man's hands move quicker in response. Should she reply? Why not? It was just research anyway, nothing was going to happen. 'I want to touch you.' Until she'd mouthed the words, Karen thought she'd made it up, but now the idea of kneading Freya's soft supple flesh filled her mind, as the stranger's hands continued to trail across her back, faster, firmer. She didn't want them to stop.

'Keep going gentlemen,' Mark moved closer to the bed. I'm going to test for results.' He slipped a finger between Freya's parted legs. 'Excellent, Freya is very wet. In fact, I would say, she was as horny as hell. You naughty girl Freya.'

Freya giggled in response. She didn't care if she was found out as a fraud; she was far too high on sensation to worry. Mark moved closer to Karen, her body tensed slightly as she felt his hand slide between her thighs and brush gently against her pussy. It was possibly the most erotic thing that had happened all evening, yet it was over in a second. 'Karen, that is also good. You're damp, not wet, but a little more work and you could be almost as rampant as the faker next to you.' Mark sounded more amused than annoyed that his class was being abused.

'Tony,' Mark addressed the man at Freya's feet. 'I would like you to try this. I believe Freya would benefit from a modicum of punishment for her bad behaviour.'

From her position on the bed Karen couldn't see what Mark handed Tony, but the wide hungry eyes that lay next to her, told Karen that the extra attention would be more than welcome, even if it hurt.

The crack echoed around the room, only drowned out by Freya's yelp, as a whip connected with her buttocks. After two more strokes, Mark announced that he felt confident they could leave Tony and Freya to amuse themselves.

Karen was pulled up by her partner, who quietly introduced himself as Sam, and was led to one of the sofas. Sam's erection was like an iron rod and Karen wasn't sure he would be able to wait much longer before his self-control broke.

Mark obviously had the same thought as, after seeing Sam's discomfort said, 'Amy I think we may be able to help both Karen and Sam. Would you come here please?'

Amy instantly obeyed, her own arousal also apparent. She knelt before Mark. *So, master and servant.'* Karen thought to herself, mentally tucking the information away for her report.

'I think Karen may benefit from a show, I suspect she likes to watch more than join in.'

Despite the warmth of the room, Karen felt herself go cold. Was Mark right? If that was true, then why did she fail to react when she watched sex shows and other hot action for work?

'Sit next to me, Karen.' Mark patted the seat next to him on the sofa. 'Amy, I would like you to lie down on the cushions please.' He continued with his instructions as Amy gratefully sunk onto the floor. 'Legs wide please, that's right. Now Sam, I would like to see how you tongue a woman.'

Sam's face coloured, but he swiftly knelt to his task and, probably enjoying his public display, began to slowly pass his tongue around Amy's distended nub. Mark nodded approvingly. 'You see,' he said to Karen companionably. 'Sam is using short neat touches, swirling around and around her clit without actually touching it. That way the tension builds up and, before long, Amy will be willing to do almost anything just to feel his tongue on her clit.'

She knew all this; she'd seen it a dozen times before. Men on women, women on women, yet, here, now, it felt different. It was all vaguely patronising and was certainly staged, but Karen was aware that she was willing the couple before her on. Karen's breath caught as she waited to see if Amy would beg for more attention or if Mark would order a change in position first.

As Karen sat naked next to her instructor, watching Amy begin to writhe on the floor, Mark stretched out a hand and slid it between her legs. Karen felt her body judder as Mark began to copy Sam's tongue movements with a single finger.

Without halting his own activity, Mark barked an order, his voice showing the first signs of personal strain. 'Stop please Sam.' Amy groaned as he moved his tongue away. 'On all fours please Amy. Sam, take her from behind.'

Sam pounced on the young woman almost before she was in position. Karen jumped as Mark began to flick his finger against her nub, whilst her eyes were still fixed on the couple in front of her. He increased his pace and inserted a finger up inside her. He whispered into her ear. 'You're wet.' Karen felt proud and surprised. 'I think you're enjoying the watching.'

Without looking at him, she replied, 'I am enjoying the attention whilst I watch.'

Mark nodded, his face suddenly full of the need he'd been suppressing all night. 'Would you like to touch her?'

Karen considered whilst she watched Amy's breasts swinging beneath her body as Sam pumped himself into her. 'Yes. I think I would.'

'Then crawl beneath her and suck her tits.'

Karen surprised herself by the speed in which she moved, she was wet, she was turned on, and she was desperate to taste the firm globes that hung before her. Lying on her back on the floor, she wriggled under Amy and, without allowing herself time to think, planted her lips around Amy's right nipple and a hand around her left, causing Mark's assistant to howl out in bliss.

Karen hadn't been playing with Amy's chest for long, when she felt a tongue between her own legs. She moaned into her mouthful of flesh, unsure if it was Mark, or if Tony and Freya had joined them on the floor. She didn't care. Heat rose within her as Amy finally shuddered out her release, and flopped down onto the luxury carpet.

There was barely a pause before Mark pulled Amy aside and climbed on top of Karen, filling her with his ready cock, smashing heavy kisses onto her face. Karen greedily kissed back, only vaguely aware that the others were watching.

As the first stirrings of an orgasm rushed through her legs into her chest and across her body, Karen opened her eyes and looked straight into the face of Freya, who dragged her away from Mark and began to nibble at her sensitive chest, making her cry out in long suppressed ecstasy.

The taxi ride home passed in a blur. Karen's head spun. How was she ever going to write about that without bearing her own soul on the page? She could still feel Mark's soft fingers against her flesh, Freya's biting teeth against her nipples, and the wondrous flow of the climax that had shaken her long frigid body.

As the cab pulled up outside her home, Karen noticed that someone was waiting on her door step. It was Charles.

'What are you doing here?'

'You promised to call when it was over, it's 2am. I wanted to make sure you were safe.'

Karen looked carefully at her boss. 'I'm fine thanks. It was very interesting.'

'Really?' Charles eyes twinkled as he watched her nipples poke through her cashmere sweater. 'How was Mark?'

'He was…Oh God, you know him don't you?' Karen coloured as the penny dropped. He had set her up for more than the report.

Charles had the decency to look slightly abashed. 'I hoped it would help you.' He moved a little closer to her. 'Would you like to share your experiences with me? I could help you work out what you're going to write.'

Karen smiled despite her indignation at being tricked. Her thighs aching with renewed need. 'I think that would be a good idea Charles. Come inside, I'll tell you all about it.'

CHAPTER ELEVEN

When the stories begin to run dry, or when I simply can't think of an original way of saying 'he stuck his dick up her pussy', I call on Kit. That isn't her real name of course, but she tells me it'll serve her purpose for now.

As fake blonde Americans go, Kit has more savvy than the average contender, yet I still keep expecting to read about her untimely death in the paper. This girl likes to sail so close to the sun that she'd give Icarus nightmares.

We met at a strip club where I was doing some research. Kit had been sat, perfectly turned out, at the bar talking to the owner. Her body language screamed professional. She was obviously working but I was intrigued about her life and asked if I could buy her a drink. I was honest with her, always the best course of action when dealing with escorts, and explained what sort of stories I collected and what sort of research material I was after.

After requesting an over-priced Vodka, Kit said, 'Tonight's kinda slow. You wanna know how I started?'

Tequila

She couldn't actually remember how she'd got there. Heat reflected off her neck as she lifted her heavy head from the damp street. It couldn't be morning already.

Her throat burned. Tequila. What a fucking stupid drink. Her tongue was stuck to her mouth; hair straggled across her face. She looked like a drugged up hooker. All she needed now was a cop car to turn up and life would be complete.

Rising slowly on her shaky legs, she brushed her grit covered palms across her ripped white skirt. Grasping the nearest wall Kit held her breath, swallowing down the bile that was building in her throat.

The world swam for a while before she took in the small row of boarded up or battered shops across the street. Kit spat into the gutter to try and escape the bad taste in her mouth. 'Jackshit Town', Kit groaned as her headache seeped through her whole body. Surely it had all been a bad dream? She rolled up her sleeves. Not a dream then. The thick bruises that adorned each wrist had already turned purple, and, judging by their yellow edges, would be multicoloured before too long.

'Perhaps you'll pay your debts from now on.' The voice growled rather than spoke. He held out his hand. Kit shuddered and turned away.

'Don't be a fool girl. You are in no fit state to go anywhere.' He towered over her, his own clothes as filthy as hers. 'I'll hold you up. Come on, you need coffee.'

Kit began to tug against his grip. She knew exactly how he'd got so dirty, and struggled to get free as he hooked a giant hand under her armpit and propelled her towards the joke of a café at the end of the street. 'Let go you bastard. Just let go!!'

'Ok.' He stopped in the middle of the road and let go of her. She crumpled and hit the deck. 'Do I prove my point?'

'Whatever.' Kit wasn't even sure why she cared. After all, surely the worst had happened. She'd worked off her debt. After surviving that she wasn't sure why the hell she was worried about being taken for coffee. He was alone; that in itself was an improvement on last night.

As she sat down on the cracked plastic chair she watched him order two black coffees and an extra espresso. The shadeless light cast a feeble beam around the room. Kit's fingers landed in one of the various sticky patches on the table. Gross. She knew she needed to eat soon, but she was damn sure she couldn't bring herself to eat here.

'You enjoyed last night, didn't you.' He spoke as though it was an undeniable fact.

'What!' She spat the word. 'I had no fuckin' choice did I!'

'You could've paid Mickey.'

'With what exactly?'

He stared at her. Her roots were beginning to show, she wasn't as blonde as she pretended to be, and the clothes she wore weren't quite designer. '*Knock- offs*,' he thought.

'You should turn tricks.' His eyes were looking beyond her clothes now. She felt as though she was being x-rayed.

'I didn't enjoy it.' Kit realised she sounded sulky, like a spoilt teenager. 'I had no choice, not if I wanted to stay alive.'

They sat in silence. Kit downed her espresso after a few mouthfuls of her accompanying Americano. It felt bitter, and she had to gag to stop herself throwing it back up again.

'You enjoyed it.' It was said as a final statement. This time she didn't argue.

Kit looked at her companion more carefully. Not her usual type, but then her usual type always screwed her over in the end. This guy had screwed her over already, or at least his mate had; he'd simply joined in. 'I'm hungry, where can I get cheap food?'

'Here?' He gestured to the smudged blackboard declaring fat with everything.

'Not here.'

'Okay, but there isn't anywhere else. You are coming home with me.' He pulled his bulky frame out of the sticky plastic seat and walked to the door. She followed. Why not?

His flat was not as bare as she would have thought it might have been, but what amazed her most was how clean and tidy it was. He smiled at her obvious surprise. 'You expected a re-run of that craphole we just had coffee in perhaps?'

'Yes. You don't give the impression of being house-proud.' Kit regarded his unkempt appearance and tried to square it with the men from last night; but last night, she had to admit, was very much a jumble of sounds, faces and discomfort. Kit couldn't honestly have said what part he'd played.

She had owed rent to the guy that owned the dump she lived in. The dump she existed in would be a better description. He'd warned her, but still she hadn't been able to get enough money together. So he'd told her she had to pay another way, before he "dealt with the situation." Kit knew his reputation and seriously did not want to know what that meant, so she'd done as he instructed and walked into town.

Sat at the bar smashing back Tequila shots, she'd guessed what would happen next; but hadn't wanted to acknowledge the fact until it actually did, just in case, by some miracle her landlord had developed a hitherto unseen nice side. No chance.

He'd had a sickeningly false smile when he finally came in. 'This way.' He picked her up by the elbow and propelled her into the pool room. There were at least six guys around the edge of the poorly lit table, maybe more. They looked at her with pure greed. '*You knew this would happen.*' She spoke to herself as she was shoved onto the table. '*You can take it.*'

'There'll be no need for restraints,' her landlord addressed the room, 'as she is not so stupid as to try an escape. However, I like restraints, so she's gonna have them anyway.' Kit shivered as the men cheered, grabbing her wrists and binding them to the pool table with rope. Her stomach leapt, was she going to throw? No, she was damn sure she wouldn't give them the satisfaction.

Her white skirt and knickers were ripped from her. Kit heard someone gob onto their hands, and felt the bile rise again as the contents was smeared between her legs. The spit felt warm against her shaking body. Stubby fingers pushed roughly against her. He laughed whoever he was. 'She's wet, the little bitch is turned on.'

The men roared around her, as zippers unleashed their contents. When the first cock skewered her cunt she screamed, more in relief that they'd started than pain. The sooner it began, the sooner it would end. 'Silence her!' the landlord had yelled, as a thick set man sat across Kit's chest, his hands kneading her tits whilst he pumped his dick between her lips, almost crushing the breath from her body.

Kit lost count of how many cocks she'd sucked; of how many men had spunked their load inside her. Life became a whirl of dicks, sweat and grunts until, suddenly, they stopped. The abrupt silence was almost eerie as they quietly stepped away. She could feel her breath thudding in her ears. Her arms were still stretched to capacity, and every inch of her ached from being moulded into any position they'd desired.

'More Tequila?' The landlord dribbled the sharp liquid over her dry lips. She choked as it slipped down her throat. 'You are very wet.' His hands began to stroke her hammered cunt. 'What do you think?' He turned back to the gang who'd just banged his tenant. 'Shall we let her come?'

They jeered their consent, and bets were quickly taken as to how long she'd last. The landlord grasped her arse and hoisted it up as high as the restraints allowed. Then, with one long slow lick from his disgusting mouth he sent her shuddering against the table. Kit no longer cared about their chants of success as she shook with satisfaction. She'd survived.

He put a plate of cheese on toast in front of her with a large glass of ice-cold water. She smiled gratefully and took a mouthful. It was delicious; she felt like she hadn't eaten for weeks. He watched her chew in silence. She noticed that he hadn't made anything for himself. She couldn't work out why he was doing this for her. Surely not guilt?

'Last night?' she said as she pushed the crumby plate away.

'Yes?'

'Which one were you?' She looked into her remaining water. 'It was a bit of a blur.'

He took her glass away and looked at her dark eyes. 'Does it matter?'

'I think it does.' She gestured around the room. 'I wouldn't have said that any of the pack of wolves that fell on me last night would live in anything other than self-inflicted squalor, except Mickey of course who probably has servants. I'm damn sure they would've seen me in the gutter and left me there. They would probably just have laughed, not offered me coffee.'

'You may be right.' He came around the table and picked up her left arm and examined her wrists. 'These are bad, come with me.'

The small bathroom to which he led her had a musty smell, as if the shower had been used frequently, but no allowance had been made for the resulting damp air to escape, forcing it to cling to the grey tiles like perspiration.

He collected a tube of arnica from a high shelf. 'Put your wrists out.' Kit obeyed and felt the warmth of his hands as the cream soothed her bruises which, on closer examination, seemed to have been very close to having full blown rope burns appearing on top of them.

'You want a shower?'

'What? Oh, thanks, but I should go.' Kit felt uneasy, something in her stirred. The sudden realisation that she was attracted to this guy was worrying. How could she be, after what he and his mates had put her through? Maybe she was just grateful and was on automatic, maybe she just felt she should offer him some kind of reward; sex usually covered it. Yet Kit instinctively felt that he would be insulted if he knew that was how she felt.

'It won't hurt to have a shower. You look done in, not to mention grubby. I'll leave you to it then.'

'You're dirty too.'

'True. I'll have one afterwards.' He passed her a large soft bath towel, pressed the shower's on button and walked out, closing the door behind him.

As she peeled off her skirt and blouse, reflecting on her lost knickers, Kit couldn't help thinking about what he'd said. Had she enjoyed it? The thought was not a comfortable one. The water began to bounce off her shoulders, neck and hair. She always had liked it rough, she was honest enough to admit that to herself, and being bound was hardly new, but last night? It had been brutal.

Kit closed her eyes as the water burned through her, and tried to sort out the sequence of events that had taken place. The calloused hands, the sickly smell of come and sweat, the grime of the room, the scratch of the baize against her back and the strain in her arms. Despite herself, Kit felt her nipples hardening; all those hands. Sure she'd been scared stiff, but while she wasn't convinced she'd actually enjoyed it, Kit knew in her heart that she hadn't hated it either. Maybe she did belong in the gutter.

She began to dry herself on the clean, if slightly discoloured, towel. Her clothes looked even more uninviting now that her body was clean. Kit dropped the towel and looked at herself in the mirror that stretched across one wall. There were bruises forming across her thighs now, and from the way her arse ached she guessed more were on the way.

Her hands began to trace the line of her areoles, and she sighed quietly as she watched the nipples of her reflection spring to life. She lightly brushed her hands over them, sending small quivers down through her body to her naked snatch. Closing her eyes Kit remembered how good it had felt to have his chunky fingers rub cream into her wounds. He had been unexpectedly tender.

The heat of the shower had begun to dissipate and she shivered as her wet hair dripped down her back. Kit wrapped the towel around her body and began to rub herself vigorously.

She was so engrossed in drying her legs that the knock on the door startled her. 'Are you okay in there?'

'I'm just drying, you can come in' She pulled the towel tighter around her.

'I'll wait till you're dressed.'

'My clothes are damp and ruined. I'm wearing a towel, so you can come in.'

'I'll wait.' His voice had developed an edge to it, but she carried on recklessly.

'You've already seen me in a far worse state for God's sake. Come in.'

'I'm not a fucking saint woman!' He yelled at the door.

'Neither am I, so get your arse in here.' Kit wasn't sure how she had come to that decision, but she knew she was as horny as hell and he was there. The mere thought of shagging him and possibly being able to work out which one he'd been in the melee of arms and cocks last night was too good an opportunity to pass up.

The haste with which he came through the door made her smile. Kit found her towel wrenched away and his thick hands encasing her breasts before she'd even drawn breath. 'Are you sure?' His voice was husky and a glance at his trousers told her exactly what he wanted to do right now.

'I'm sure,' she whispered up into her ear, before nipping it between her teeth.

He roared and pushed her into the mirror, squashing her tits against the steamed up glass. He poked a finger up her ass, which sucked back at him greedily. His groan of lust as he realised that she was up for an arse fucking made Kit weak at the knees.

So much had happened to her battered body in the last twenty-four hours, she suddenly wasn't sure if she had the strength to give as good as she got, but her clit already felt slick and the familiar need was welling up inside her stomach.

'There's no fuckin' room in here.' He picked her up under one arm and carried her to his bed. Throwing her down, he positioned her so that her bruised and rounded arse pointed into the air.

Standing in front of her face he released his cock, and teased it against her parted lips, before letting her engulf him in her mouth. After a few seconds, he pulled out, leaving her wanting and empty, but giving him enough of her spit to lubricate his dick.

He knelt behind her and kissed the pulsating rim of her bum hole, then, with only a second's hesitation, he drove his cock between her cheeks. Kit screamed as his thick shaft ripped her skin in its need for more room. He showed no concern. He was up her arse channel and that was all that mattered. As he jerked himself off, finally creaming inside her, he cried out with pent up desire.

Once he'd pulled out of her panting, tear stained body, he knelt again and, pulling a handkerchief out of a draw, he dabbed Kit's wounded arse. Then, with contrasting tenderness, he turned her over and slowly, carefully, licked her wet pussy until her cries of pain became whimpers of satisfaction.

He cradled Kit in his arms. 'So, did you like that?'

'I did.' She met his gaze without shame.

'I knew you would. I couldn't believe that a woman who could willingly endure last night couldn't take me too.'

'You mean, I didn't have you last night?'

He smiled, 'I think you should lay off the Tequila love. I'm just the bloody barman; and I still think you should turn tricks.'

CHAPTER TWELVE

After my initial meeting with Kit, we became friends. Not close friends or anything- I don't think Kit does close. Yet she quickly became a source of research and information about clients she'd known, and the experiences of the women she's encountered in the course of her work.

Once such girl, who I'll call Bess (Kit had forgotten her name - if she ever even knew it) had an ex-boyfriend who was big on objects of intrusion, in particular stilettos, as the next two short sharp stories will illustrate.

Bad Behaviour

'If we were still together, do you think the sex would be that good?' he asked, as the scene on the television picture flashed to three women fucking each other against a fridge.

'Better.' Bess looked him straight in the eye.

'Better?' His mouth twitched. 'Are you still a bad girl then?'

'Would I be sat watching porn with you if I wasn't?' Bess slowly undid her blouse as she spoke, revealing naked tits, which she immediately began to stroke. 'Bad, dirty, and very,very naughty.'

'In that case,' he said as his eyes narrowed, 'take off the rest of your clothes and go upstairs.' His voice became commanding. 'Lay face down on my bed with your feet dangling off the edge. The first thing I want to see when I come through the door is your delicious arse.'

She caught the lust-driven look in his eye, nodded meekly and stripped bare before leaving the room.

Counting under his breath, he stood up and headed for the stairs. 'Six, seven...' In the hall he stopped, Bess's frighteningly high stilettos were lying where she'd kicked them off. He grabbed one and ran up the stairs. 'Ten.'

She was lying just as he'd instructed, except that her hand was between her legs and her panting told him that she was not far from bringing herself off. 'Stop right now.' He swung the stiletto down hard onto her swaying butt. 'You are a very naughty bad girl.' He struck again as she yelled out.

Pulling Bess's arms over her head, he tied them together with his belt. 'Stay.' The shoe connected with her backside again and again, until an angry red sole imprint began to form on her peach skin.

He squeezed his hand between her crotch as she squealed into the duvet. 'You really are a dirty girl aren't you?'

'Oh yes.'

'You want more?'

'Yes.'

'Yes what?' he had begun to grunt his words; primal need taking firm control of his actions.

'Yes Master, Sir, whatever! Just fuck me!' Bess shouted out as he pinched her damp flesh.

'Not yet.' The stiletto hung from his fingers. 'Nice shoe, you don't mind if I try it on do you?' He slipped it over his erection and walked towards her face. 'Stand up bitch.'

Bess scrambled to her feet, her face flushed with longing as she looked at the shoe. He smiled 'Suck me off.' Swiftly, she knelt before him and attempted to engulf his cock, but he pushed her back. 'No. Just the shoe.'

It only took a split second of uncertainty before Bess greedily turned her attention to the sharp black heel, treating it just as if it was his hard dick.

With a deep groan he shoved her away, forcing her onto all fours on the bed. Grasping her arse, he plunged himself between her butt cheeks.

'Bite pillow baby,' he cried as he jammed the stilettos thin heel into her cunt.

'Scream dirty girl,' he ordered.

So she did.

The Candle Holder

As Bess watched, the wax started to dribble down the heel of the red stiletto. It had taken an agonising eternity for the flame to start melting the candle wedged into her shoe; now, at last, it was producing a steady trickle of molten liquid.

Her eyes stung. She had been willing the candle on for so long that even when her eyes were closed, she could still see its glow.

Inwardly she'd been screaming in frustration for at least, the last twenty minutes, and Bess was grateful for her soft gag. Her tormenter had been rubbing her naked tethered body with the toe of a second stiletto for nearly an hour, and had vowed to do nothing else until the candles wax had dribbled down to the very tip of its sister shoe's sharp heel.

Bess's body shivered at the intense feeling of need that the smooth stiletto produced across her taut skin. The bed to which she was tied was dotted with sweat. So far he had avoided touching either her breasts or pussy; yet her nipples already felt like rocks and her clit was as wet and slippery as if he'd been pushing the spiked heel deep inside her.

It was his abrupt intake of breath which told her that the moment had come at last. Bess watched his shadowy outline move closer as he tore off his clothes, freeing his long restricted cock, as a drop of wax hit the shelf beneath the stiletto's razor sharp heel.

The circular motion of the shoe stopped. Bess could have cried at the withdrawal of its touch, and forced herself to bite back frustrated tears. She held her breath as she watched the flicker of the flame as he picked up the candle-filled stiletto. Holding it between her tits, he highlighted their curves with the orange heat and light against the darkness of the room.

Bess had not been prepared for the stinging pain as he swung the sole of the second shoe across her aching breasts. The gag was no longer enough to prevent her noisy response.

His erection swayed menacingly as he maintained the attack whilst re-directing the flame to between her outstretched and fastened legs. Bess braced herself as the sole smacked hard against her distended cunt. Heat swept through her as she gave in to the beautiful agony.

As he silently repeated the assault, Bess saw him rub the stiletto's wax coated heel up and down his dick. It was too much. Bess's body began to spasm in its restraints, all self-control gone.

He fell across his prisoner, sliding into her stickiness. Dropping the second shoe, he ripped the gag out of her panting mouth and replaced it with the wax-coated stiletto heel, which she sucked hungrily.

He watched her for a second, bound and deliciously wanton, writhing in the stiletto's light before, at last, he buried himself into her beautiful trapped and bucking body.

Chapter Thirteen

Just because a coffee shop has table clothes and sugar lumps rather than wipe down surfaces and damp sugar sachets, doesn't mean it is always the location of respectable and high-brow conversation.

In the Oxfordshire town of Wantage there are several nice cafés and tea shops. I was in such an establishment late one Friday afternoon, opposite a table at which sat a dark haired, pale skinned woman, who I'd estimate to be in her late-thirties. She was detachedly sipping at her cappuccino, obviously waiting for someone to join her. Her manner was so unsettled and her glances towards the door were so frequent that my curiosity was roused.

Just in case a story was about to emerge, I ordered myself a second Americano and opened my notebook.

I didn't have to wait long before a second woman, of a similar age, joined the first. The newcomer barely had time to sit down with her pot of tea before the first woman, somewhat flustered, and yet also elated, launched into her tale.

I couldn't help but overhear.

Untouched

'But we can't, we mustn't.'

Jon smiled down at Mae, an arrogant look in his eyes. 'As I understand it,' he poured another glass of wine and passed it across to her, 'the deal is that no other man or woman must touch you.'

'Marriage is rather more than that.' Mae tried and failed to avoid eye contact.

'Of course it is, but physically, I'm right aren't I.'

Mae could feel her heart thudding against her rib cage. She answered slowly, aware she was already in too deep. 'You could be…if you wanted to be.'

Jon looked at her laid back on his sofa. It hadn't taken long to get Mae nice and relaxed, but now he'd have to proceed carefully, or all his hard work getting her to this stage would be destroyed. 'You want to don't you.' It was a statement not a question. Jon knelt next to her, breathing his words into her ear. 'Can't you remember how good it felt?'

Mae did remember, and she did want to, but she was married. On the other hand, she could easily convince herself that her husband was no saint. A task made simpler for her by the obvious electricity shooting through the air. But how could it work if Jon didn't touch her?

'You trust me don't you?' He smiled the same charming smile he'd first ensnared her with a decade ago.

'Of course I don't.' She didn't, not for a minute. Mae knew she was smiling despite herself, and privately acknowledged that in the fight between conscience and desire. Desire was ahead on points.

Jon crouched closer to her face and whispered. 'I madly want to fuck you. Shag you until you scream, until I explode inside you - but I can't, not now you're all legal, and yet…' He stood up and stepped away from her, his voice dripping with arrogant confidence. '…I can give you a damn good seeing to without laying a single finger on you, and without you laying a finger on me.'

'How on earth could…' He raised a hand, cutting her sentence short.

'The worst you can be accused of then is assisted masturbation, and who'd know anyway?'

'I'd know.' Her smile was gone, but a treacherous silent need was welling up in the pit of her stomach.

Jon stared deep into her dark blue eyes. He knew he'd won, and wanted to savour every moment of victory. 'You do what I say, and that horny body of yours will get the seeing to it so desperately needs. Yes?'

Mae didn't reply, but then she didn't need to. He'd won, he always won. She couldn't work out how this had happened. They'd only met by chance outside a local coffee shop an hour ago. It was eight years since she'd last seen Jon, yet here she was, lying flat on her back on his sofa, putty in his hands. She felt consumed with a heady mixture of shame and lust. Her mouth had gone dry, and her palms felt damp with nervous anticipation.

'I need some supplies,' Jon spoke practically, as if he was about to gather tools together to fix his car or something. 'As I'm not allowed to touch you, you'd better take your clothes off whilst I'm gone.'

Watching his retreating back, Mae felt momentarily paralysed against the soft leather sofa cushions. She shouldn't do this. He had given her the perfect opportunity to grab her handbag and run for it. Yet she stayed exactly where she was.

Closing her eyes tightly, Mae tried to feel guilty for wanting to stay, but she couldn't. She just felt sexy and desperate to be touched by a man she'd sworn she'd never even speak to again.

With trembling fingers Mae undid the buttons of her blouse, before standing and sliding off her trousers, socks and knickers. Finally, keeping her eyes firmly closed as if to deny what she was doing, Mae freed her breasts from her black satin bra.

As she lay back down, the leather felt both cool and sticky beneath her bare flesh. Mae fervently wished Jon would hurry up, but daren't open her eyes. Then it occurred to her that he may have been watching her strip all along. The idea caused her body to goose pimple all over.

'Good,' Jon's voice made Mae jump as it cut through the silence of the room. 'Keep your eyes shut and put your hands beneath your back, I don't want you moving about.'

As Mae did as he asked, she noticed that his breathing had become slightly shallow, a sure sign that Jon was extremely turned on. She wondered if he was naked too. In her mind he was. Mae could clearly visualise every inch of his tightly toned chest and his tall slim frame.

She flinched; something cold and smooth was being rubbed against her left leg. 'What's that?' Mae had to squeeze her eyelids tighter to stop them from opening and breaking the spell.

'A bottle.' Jon spoke bluntly as he continued to roll the icy bottle of juice up and down her thighs, its shiny surface making her skin flush with need and yet shiver with cold.

Just as Mae reached the point where she couldn't possible stay still any longer, he abruptly took the bottle away. Mae's groan at the passing of sensation was replaced by a yelp of shock, as a searing hot cloth was thrown onto her right breast. She was just acclimatising herself to the heat when Jon dropped an ice cold flannel onto her left teat. The juxtaposition of temperatures caused tears to spring to her eyes, as Mae struggled to keep her hands hidden and not use them to knock the wet cloths off her chest.

Moments later the flannels were levered away, Jon laughed down at her. 'I've always wondered what my kitchen tongs would come in useful for.'

The air of the room teased Mae's puckered skin until two new hot and cold flannels landed on opposite sides of her chest, and forced her to suck in her breath, hard. The effect of the clingingly damp material was almost as potent as a hot tongue lapping at her nipples, and Mae found her already slick pussy igniting in response.

She whimpered with both relief and loss, as once again Jon flicked the cloths away, dumping them onto the floor. Then, positioning the tongs over her extant right nipple, he squeezed it hard between the metal teeth.

Mae shrieked in shock, her hips lifting off the sofa in an attempt to escape the pain, before he swapped his attention to the other nipple and clamped it tightly, the tongs sharp edges cutting against her areolas.

'Jon!' Mae yelled out. 'Stop!'

'No way!' Jon's voice was gruff. 'You have no idea how fantastic you look. If you knew, you'd never want me to stop.'

After an agonising eternity, in which Mae's body flushed between the need for more pain and the wish for it to end, Jon finally abandoned her teats and began to smack the undersides of her pale breasts. Lightly at first, he worked the kitchen utensil across her belly and down her legs, avoiding the neat triangle of her snatch, which visibly quivered in response to each strike.

The obvious avoidance of her clit was driving Mae to distraction, and the desire she felt to be struck between her open legs was overwhelming. She'd never wanted to be hurt, to be punished, so badly in her life. '*Maybe*' she thought, her mind racing, '*I deserve punishment for being here.*'

She tried to divert her mind by concentrating on Jon's breathing instead, but her head swam and her back arched, as she called out, 'Please Jon. Please just do it!'

Turned on further by her begging, Jon bought the tongs down triumphantly hard against her soft mound. The assault went on and on, as he smacked her like a man possessed. Her cunt stung, and Mae longed for him to physically touch her, to crush his mouth against hers. It took all her willpower not to free her trapped hands from beneath her, and wrap her arms around his body. She was sure she hadn't said anything out loud though, maybe he'd just read her mind.

'I can't Mae, you don't belong to me,' Jon's voice was a strange mixture of regret and lust. 'But I can give you the stuffing you so badly need. Open your eyes.' Mae obeyed quickly, and saw his naked cock bouncing full and rigid before her. He was holding a dauntingly thick cucumber between his hands. 'A bit cliché perhaps, but a perfect size, don't you think?'

Mae didn't reply, she just swallowed hard at the thought of the invasion to come.

'Widen those legs.' She did as Jon ordered, and he very slowly, began to inch the green cylinder up inside her slippery opening. 'My god you're so wet, maybe I should have done this to you years ago and I might not have lost you.'

Mae couldn't respond to his uncharacteristic confession that he had lost her, and not the other way around. She was concentrating on her pussy, which already felt as if it was full to bursting, and he was still pushing, still stretching her wider to accommodate the makeshift dildo.

Finally he stopped, and her muscles clamped themselves around the blessed width. Jon grinned as Mae's body twitched despite her obvious attempts to keep still. 'I think a finishing touch is required, don't you?'

She creased her sweat prickled forehead questioningly as Jon picked up his hairbrush. 'I want you to roll off the sofa and get onto all fours.' Mae opened her mouth to protest that the cucumber would fall out, but he pre-empted her. 'I will hold the end. Don't worry, it's firmly wedged.'

Clumsily, Mae flipped down onto the beige carpet and positioned herself on her hands and knees. Was he going to smack her again? Beat her hard? The hairbrush had a wide flat head, and would certainly make a good paddle. Mae shivered again, knowing that one strike was probably all that was needed to send her into heaving throws of ecstasy.

'You are amazing.' Jon whispered the words, still holding the end of the cucumber so that her body didn't dispel it, and stood admiring the vision he'd created.

He picked up the brush and flashed it before her eyes. 'A nice wide paddle, don't you think?'

She gasped, but couldn't reply as Jon began to glide the cucumber in and out of her body, building up a maddeningly gentle rhythm. Mae's deep throated moans turned to soft purrs as the desire in her grew and grew.

Sensing she was about to come, Jon squeezed some lube onto his hands. 'However, this hairbrush also has a nice long round handle doesn't it, not too thin, not too thick, just right for...' He smeared the lube over the handle and, taking a firm hold of the brush's head, plunged it between her arse cheeks.

Mae's shocked screech resounded around the room as Jon eased the brush's handle deeper into her butt, whilst sliding the broad green dildo, faster and faster, in and out of her cunt.

Her hips bucking, Mae came in a noisy heap until she collapsed, a spent force on the floor. The cucumber fell out, but the brush remained lodged firmly in place, clenched between her buttocks.

She didn't move as a delicious but confused shame shot through her. How had he convinced her to do that? And yet, as her satiated body began to calm, Mae wondered, as she watched Jon run to shoot his load in the bathroom, and she removed her unorthodox butt-plug, how soon it might be before they could do it again.

After all, he hadn't even touched her...

CHAPTER FOURTEEN

I never found out their name. They spoke quietly and never once looked me in the eye. I have no idea how they heard about my quest for erotic experiences. I'm just very glad they found me.

Watching

Her breasts were so full that the lens on the binoculars had to be adjusted. They were more like silky smooth balloons really. Beautifully round balloons with large pert peaks that just invited an extra blow.

From this distance the watcher was unable to hear the moans and sighs that they knew would be emanating from her slightly parted lips, although they could clearly see the sweaty moisture that had gathered around her full mouth.

Lying on her back, head tilted slightly, legs flat but parted, the watcher held their breath as the blonde's manicured fingers ran over her own tits. Completely unaided, she was slowly pushing herself to the point of no return. She was obviously in no hurry, and the watcher was grateful.

Adjusting their sweat dampened clothing, the watcher pondered the contents of the showgirl's dirty mind. Perhaps she was lying on a four poster bed in a beautiful room, tied up, being beaten by a man in black. Perhaps, in her imagination, she was being rubbed up against a tree, deep within a thick forest, her perfect skin snagging against the bark. Maybe she was on all fours, a woman smothering her mouth as a penis pumped its worth between her tight butt cheeks.

The watcher switched back to the spectacle before them. It was too risky to continue with pondering the contents of the blonde's erotic peccadilloes; they didn't want to come there and then. Once again the lenses were adjusted. Wiping the perspiration from around the eye pieces, the watcher focused on the prostrate figure writhing on top of an unzipped sleeping bag.

Her hands were no longer fondling her handsome chest, but were trailing between her legs. One leg had been raised slightly and was bent at the knee, the other remained flat on the floor, hiding the sure fact that she was dipping her fingers in and out of her moist pussy. The waves of want she was creating as she massaged her distended clit were almost tangible. The watcher swallowed; their throat was as dry as hers must be as she played with her snatch.

Her movements became faster and faster, until, at last, she began to raise her hips off the floor, pushing herself hard against her own hand. A finger strayed inside her hot sticky hole and the watcher could faintly hear her initial mews of lust and satisfaction over the background noise as she brought her body towards the point of ecstasy. Then suddenly her panted gasps were clearly audible as her head rolled from side to side, her blonde hair tangling beneath her head, until at last she lay still, sated.

Start again. Start again. The watcher was silently willing her on. More, more, and they was not alone. At the back of the room the spectator stood upon an old wooden chair to achieve the best possible view, binoculars lowered, arms resting, hands sticky and weak, their own arousal began to subside a little. A drink would help. Jumping down from the chair, they weaved their way through to the bar and ordered a pint, which their parched lips gratefully welcomed.

The watcher focussed on the crowd. Many, mostly men, jostled at the front of the stage waiting for the next performance. The silent figure preferred the back. You couldn't hear much anyway above the jeers of the crowd, but a good imagination could fill in the blanks, making it more erotic than it really was, continually pushing their own fantasy laden boundaries.

The shrieks coming from the front alerted the voyeur to the blonde's return to the stage. They raced back to the chair, instantly turned on as they admired the white lace topped hold-ups encasing the firm cream legs. This was obviously a girl who worked out, and wasn't afraid of the occasional botox jab. The watcher was not complaining. Certainly not.

The sleeping bag had been cast aside, but as the blonde circled the chair that had replaced it, a neat set of zip prints could clearly be seen embedded into her skin. The lights dimmed and the thud of music hit a crescendo in the smoky room. Blue neon illuminated the stage as the woman's flirty smile seemed to aim itself at every individual in the overcrowded room.

Gyrating to the back beat that vibrated around the club, the blonde sat on the edge of the chair, legs wide, fingers displaying her vulva to the hungry crowd. This was the part of the show the watcher had been waiting for. The solo warm up was over, now she wanted a thorough seeing to and her eyes scanned the room for someone to quench her seemingly insatiable need.

Boy she was hot. The watcher focused on the hands with which she kneaded her full boobs. The girl stood up, and beckoned into the temporarily hushed crowd. A tall slim man approached her from the other side of the room.

As usual she had chosen well. Not a terribly attractive man, but well built, and judging by the bulge in his jeans, well hung. His olive skin shone with perspiration as his colleagues shouted obscene support towards the stage.

The blonde wasted no time and opened his shirt buttons, revealing a breathtakingly smooth chest, which her tongue quickly tasted, while she placed his rough hands onto her tits. This time the sigh that escaped her lips was so loud that the witness, binoculars firmly in position, felt it vibrate through their own body. The man was gorgeous. As she stripped away his denims, shoes and socks, the watcher swallowed hard. Their mind had already fixed a picture of him, bent double, a thick dick pushing between his curved buttocks. Perhaps the girl would be there too, perhaps not; that was a dream for later.

The watcher's eyes refocused. The chosen man had taken the blonde's place on the very edge of the chair. His hands were tied behind his back and his eyes were encased in a black velvet mask, completing his temporary enslavement to this creamy goddess. Once she had arranged him to her satisfaction the temptress sat astride his lap facing the audience, his fiercely erect dick poking out between her legs.

This wasn't right. She appeared to be looking for someone else. The watcher's heartbeat quickened, this was not the normal routine. She should have been on her hands and knees, her mouth working its way around her subject's cock. The change in routine was unnerving; the guy should have spunked all over her face by now.

She beckoned to a deeply tanned young woman, whose jet black tightly cropped hair framed her soft face. A nod from the blonde and she mounted the stage before stripping slowly, teasingly, returning the crowd to its accustomed frenzy of hunger and desire. Stood now in just sheer black hold-ups, she was a perfect contrast to her paler counterpart, who remained sat on the chair behind her. *So*, thought the watcher, *this has been planned. It's okay.* Breathing a sigh of relief, they relaxed and prepared to enjoy the forthcoming visual feast.

The blonde got off the man's lap and turned to the new female. The electricity between the women was almost visible as they attacked each other's mouths with furious need. The audience's taunts were obviously turning them on further as they stroked and kneaded each others breasts, totally ignoring the captive man behind them. The observer delighted in imagining his confusion. He must be aware that some action was going on in front of him, but was frustratingly unable to join in.

The blonde laid herself back on the floor, but this time the tanned girl quickly joined her. Head to snatch, each greedily licked out the other. The watcher could hear hasty wagers being taken all around as fellow voyeurs lay bets on who would come first.

Sticky liquid ran freely down the girls quivering legs as their saliva mixed with their pussy juices. They were moving their hands across each other with increasing pace; their tongues quickening, each trying to control themselves, whilst attempting to make the other come. Mewls began to emanate from the blonde's mouth, as despite herself, her incredible body lost the battle and shivered with both satisfaction and defeat.

Leaving her partner panting on the ground, the black haired girl stood and made her way to the waiting man, finally rewarding him for his patience by placing a pair of firm lips around his rigid dick. The watcher sighed and adjusted the binoculars so that they could better view the tongue that was licking the beautiful cock as if it was an exquisite ice cream.

Just as the tone of the man's cries told the room he was about to explode, the dark haired girl turned to face her audience, before sheathing his cock, sitting astride him and jamming the thick width up inside her. Grinding up and down wildly, her face crunched up in release as they both exploded to the delighted whoops of crowd.

Not to be outdone, the blonde rose from her place on the floor, and kneeling in front of her friend, pushed her back so that she lent heavily onto the man, his penis still trapped inside her. The sight of the freshly exposed clit through the lenses was almost too much for the watcher as they witnessed the blonde circle her tongue slowly around the perfect nub, until the dark girl's contented sigh made the bound man yell out in discomfort beneath her.

The watcher's arms ached with the tension of keeping still, and her body ached from not being allowed to respond to the show she had been watching so closely. She could no longer ignore her own desires as she heard the roar of the man on stage, who'd been released to fall upon the women who had made him their willing prisoner.

Cradling her beloved binoculars, she pushed through the crush, making her way outside as quickly as possible. She was very aware of the dampness that had spread between her legs and stuck her satin knickers against her mound. The flat was very close, and her breathing quickened as she fumbled for her door keys.

Throwing her belongings to the floor, her tight fitting jeans and cropped top were swiftly discarded. Looking at her reflection in the mirror, the red haired girl smiled as she pulled down her knickers, and stood simply in white lace topped hold-ups. With a last look at her own unbound chest, she lay down on the sleeping bag she had placed on the floor earlier.

Closing her eyes, she allowed herself the attention her frustrated body so desperately desired…

CHAPTER FIFTEEN

Some years ago, when I was still respectable, I went to university. Whilst I was there, I made the best friends I've ever had, one of whom is still heavily embroiled in student life. Over the past ten years Jack has worked his way from one degree to another, determined to put off entering the "real world" for as long as possible.

Recently we had one of our regular coffee trips together, to catch up on all the gossip. One look at Jack, a broad smile plastered across his face, his deep blue eyes twinkling as he sipped his coffee, and I knew he had a story to tell. Being one of my greatest supporters, he was more than willing to help me note down his adventure.

Crushed

The general din from the concert behind me had reached such a level of confusion that hand signals were now the only possible means of communication. As I slowly inched closer to the bar, I began to wonder how on earth I'd get our drinks back through the heaving mass of people.

Thankful that I wasn't claustrophobic, I slowly shuffled along with the crowd. I could still move my arms but otherwise I was almost totally immobilised. For some unseen reason we had all come to a complete stop. Being above average height gave me the advantage of spotting potential "sliding into gaps" opportunities, but eventually I had to accept that I was going nowhere fast, and was destined to remain thirsty for some time.

I looked around at my temporary colleagues. Apart from hair colour, and a stab at gender, I couldn't really tell you much about the people who were standing so close to me that we knew what the sides of each others legs felt like.

My mind started to wander. A thirty or so deep crowd of people, all piling in one direction – what were they all thinking? How many pockets had been picked? How many people were accidentally on purpose feeling up the person in front of them?

I began to imagine how I'd react if a strange pair of hands started to stroke my arse as I stood there, unable to move, my protests going unheard. My hands began to itch as I turned my attention to the person directly in front of me. Female, above average height, bright red hair in tidy bunches, short skirt; older than eighteen I guessed, perhaps younger than twenty-five.

I was so close to her that as I looked down I had an excellent view of the top of her head. My crotch was already lightly rubbing against her flimsy skirted rear, and the urge to put my hands over her shoulders and slide them down onto her breasts (which my imagination had decided would be both full and firm), was overwhelming.

I still can't believe I did it. What if she'd screamed? I'd have been arrested for sure, if anyone should have had heard her.

I would like to be able to say I'd been tentative and gentle; testing the water. But I was straight on, squeezing her tits hard (which were actually small, but beautifully tight). I felt her body stiffen as her attempts to instantly turn around were inhibited by the general crush. I tensed, expecting a slap across my kneading digits. It didn't come. Instead her body shuffled within its confined space, her own hands slipping behind her and flipping up her short skirt to reveal a pair of neat pale buttocks encased in lace knickers, which she pushed against my hard confined dick.

I must confess to a moment of panic then. What if we were spotted? Her intentions were obviously as impure as my own. I took a deep breath to calm myself; there was no way any extra pushing could be viewed as odd. For all I knew, the entire crowd could have been at it. The only person who may have been more suspicious than the rest was the guy behind me. As I pulled back slightly from this amazing girl, I could feel his cock was also hard. Or was I simply imagining it?

Wriggling one hand down between her arse and my denims I undid my flies and freed my cock. She must have known what I was doing as she instantly pressed back harder, standing on her toes to feel my length better against her buttocks.

I eased the delicate lace knickers to one side and rubbed myself against her rounded flesh. Her hands snaked around behind her and she grabbed my tip with expert fingers. I tried to suppress a groan, but failed, and anxiously looked around at the still oblivious crowd, as her fingers grasped the end of my shaft.

I have no idea how I kept such an impassive expression on my face. A total stranger was wanking me against her bum, and my head was full of the picture we must be creating. What's more, each time she forced me back fractionally I brushed against the anonymous guy behind me. I swear he was getting harder all the time and I longed to be able to include him in our secret sex.

I guess I became reckless then, because as she smoothed my dick I began to push back harder. All the time I was waiting to be found out, waiting for a cry of protest. None came.

Grateful of her perfect height, I slipped a hand down as far as I could; feeling between her legs, fingering her slippery wetness. Perhaps she was wearing high heels, I couldn't tell.

I knew I couldn't hang on much longer. Sandwiched between this horny girl and a hard man, I thought I'd explode with the thought of the situation alone. Knocking her hand away, I notched my shaft against her. Biting my tongue to conceal the noise rising in my throat, I eased into her; each time making sure the guy behind knew exactly what was happening. I longed for him to put a hand around me, to feel for himself how well my cock fitted inside this willing woman. He didn't, but the idea of it was the final straw, and I quickly filled her with my come.

As I pulled out (not easy in the limited space), I could just see the first trickle of my liquid as it began to run down her legs, before she daintily pulled her knickers back into place and recovered herself with the little green skirt.

The crowd had hardly moved. I don't suppose the whole thing had taken more than five minutes, but it sure made waiting for that pint a whole lot more interesting.

I hadn't really thought about the people to the side of us; I am still not sure whether they knew what had happened or not; if they did, no one said anything.

When I finally did reach the bar, the girl had long since been lost in the crush ahead of me, but a friendly voice from behind offered to buy me a drink, and quietly thanked me for making his wait in the queue so enjoyable.

CHAPTER SIXTEEN

It is frequently the anonymity of a situation that adds a certain spice to an unexpected encounter with a stranger.

Two of the bar staff working at one of Oxford's student dominated night spots, have taken the anonymous erotic interlude, and developed it into an art form.

Break Time

The temperature dropped as the door closed behind them. He hesitated for a moment before following them further into the club's store. Seconds later he was being pulled across the dark room onto a huge pile of empty cardboard boxes which lay discarded in the far corner. He could feel his cock stirring beneath his jeans. So far they had not spoken. They hadn't needed to.

The blonde was laughing. Her eyes laughed first, just ahead of her lips, which were moist with anticipation. The boxes crunched slightly as they were squashed beneath their combined weight. The thumping of the dance floor, only a corridor away, was almost drowned out by the ticking of the storeroom clock.

The girls, still anonymous, looked at each other, and with an unspoken signal they acted. Pulling off their t-shirts they revealed two sets of perfect tits. The red head's rich mouth was nuzzling at her partners nipples before their guest had time to react to the wonderful, unbelievable, sight. Then she turned the blonde towards him. 'She's yours for the taking'. She smiled teasingly. 'If you want her? You'll have to decide quickly though, we only have a half hour break.'

He'd seen them watching him from the other side of the bar as they served his fellow clubbers. When they approached him, each taking a hand and guiding his slim frame towards what they called "a safe place", he couldn't believe it. He wasn't sure whether he should resist or not, so he thought he'd see what happened next. Anyway, his mates were watching.

Somehow he couldn't move. His brain was screaming at his body to work. To grab her, lick her neat breasts, and release her hips from her short black skirt, but he simply stood there, mesmerised.

The red head shrugged and, moving behind her friend, grasped her nipples between bronzed fingers. As her taught skin was expertly rubbed, the blonde's head fell back onto her comrade's shoulders, her eyes closed in pleasure.

'She loves this. Why don't you try it?' Still he couldn't move, but his eyes never left them. The red head, who was obviously relishing her currant dominance, started to kiss the blonde. Big, deep, probing kisses; first on the mouth, then down her neck, whilst her fingertips continued to brush the almond tips.

It was the blonde's yell that woke him up. As she came there, right in front of him, under the careful ministrations of another girl, he realised that this wasn't just another fantasy. This was everything he wanted. It was real.

As if sensing that he'd come to a positive decision, the red head pulled a condom out of her mini-skirts pocket and threw it at him. He inclined his head, and posted it into his jeans pocket.

The blonde almost sagged with relief as he tore off his shirt, closely followed by her skirt. He pushed her back into the red head's arms, spread her knicker-free legs, and greedily lapped up the juice which ran down the inside of her thighs. Her arms reached up, and her fingers dug into his short dark hair to steady herself. His dick ached, but he wasn't ready to take his jeans off. He couldn't be sure how much control he'd have without their restraining presence.

Glancing up from his intense work around her clit, he could see she was very close, but he didn't want to be the one to trigger her second orgasm. He was in charge now, and he wanted to watch.

The red head staggered a little as he pulled her roughly towards him. 'Finish her off,' he ordered.

'Certainly Sir.' She spoke with mock gravity, and knelt down, sliding two perfectly manicured fingers inside her friends soaking snatch. He watched as the fingers moved slowly, rhythmically in and out, making tiny slurping noises in time to the clock. He stepped forward and began to kiss the red head on the neck, her face and her stomach. He circled all around her chest without actually touching it, planting the lightest of touches on her belly and her arms, forcing a groan from her confident mouth. He knew the need for attention in her breast must be almost unbearable. Would she beg? No; too proud. He suspected that right now she would like to though.

The tension was cut abruptly as the blonde cried out once more, her body shivering in satisfaction. The red head pulled away from him and stuffed an aching tit into her friend's mouth, who instantly obliged by flicking her skilful tongue over the neglected nipple. Red's murmur of relief became a sigh of pleasure when he thrust his hard cock between her pink lips.

He had dreamt about this sort of thing, but the reality of the situation was almost too much. The girls so busy together, combined with the tongue expertly, divinely, licking at his tip, was driving him to distraction. He withdrew hastily and took a deep breath, gathering himself.

The clock ticked. The red head was whimpering for more attention. He glanced at the cardboard bed beneath him; it was more or less squashed flat now. Time must be short and he was desperate to be inside one of them. He didn't care which one.

Ripping the condom out of its packaging and rolling it into place, he lay on his back, his discomfort soon forgotten as his shaft was quickly swallowed up as the blonde sat astride him. The delicious sensations that coursed through him doubled as the red head lowered herself onto his face, offering her pussy to his open mouth.

The stifled mews and groans from above told him that the girls were kissing each other as one pumped against his cock, and one rocked against his tongue. He held red's thighs tightly, feeling the

101

pleasing weight mould into him. Perhaps their hands were busy working on each others tits. He was sure they would be.

It was a thought too far, and suddenly he pushed the red head away, crying out his release as he shot his load into the blonde above him. As he moved away, panting hard, the girls wasted no time in fingering themselves to their own climax, giving him one last memorable spectacle.

Tick. The girls were bar staff again. Collecting their clothes from the jumble of cardboard, they hastened towards the door. Turning to him for a final look, he blew them a kiss, admiring their calm, but rather crumpled, appearance. Tomorrow he would have to pinch himself. Had that really just happened?

The backs of his long legs ached where they had been rubbed against the uneven surface, and they were already bruising. It had happened, and he was about to develop the marks to prove it.

CHAPTER SEVENTEEN

I adore the bus. The tube is often more convenient, but on the less intimidating atmosphere of the bus, a previously unfamiliar person can, with a little encouragement, be unwittingly coerced into telling you the most intimate secrets of their lives. You are also less likely to have your conversation abruptly curtailed by the sudden arrival at your confidant's destination.

It had been a number eight bus on which I met Ellie, on her way home from a very interesting day at work. I had to physically restrain myself from bringing out a notebook as I listened to my co-passenger. In fact I got off the bus a stop earlier than I intended so I could scribble down Ellie's tale before it lost any of its potency.

Cupboard Lust

She had only spilt the coffee for God's sake. What the hell would have happened if she'd crashed the computer or something?

The cupboard was cramped. Ellie felt the cool grey metal shelves dig into her ribs as her face crushed a pile of envelopes. Her smart black trousers were already rumpled around her ankles. She jumped as she felt cold metal slide between her hot legs and her French knickers. Scissors; Ellie's mind raced as she felt her underwear being cut away.

So far nothing had been said. Ellie knew that when he'd marched her into the stationery cupboard, her arm twisted up her back, she should have struggled and protested, but somehow she'd felt compelled to move with him. She wanted to see if the expression across his gruff face was simply anger, or if she really had seen a frisson of lust cross his dark features.

'No question about that now' Ellie thought, as she trembled beneath the force of his left hand which pressed into the small of her back, pinning her in place. His other hand was pushing between her parted legs, cupping her snatch, squeezing her wet flesh. Ellie could hear the soft slurping sound her pussy made as her squeals of discomfort and rising hunger were stifled by the stationery in front of her.

He grunted into her neck, his fingers working sharply as he took it in turns to jab them into both her snatch and her thin arsehole. Ellie drooled into the envelopes as her body responded to his thrusts. First pushing back onto his hand, feeling her stomach churn at the unaccustomed invasion, before plunging forward, her cunt consuming another finger, until she was pre-empting his moves and working in time with his hand.

His coarse breath quickened and he turned her around so abruptly that she almost tripped over her trousers. Forcing Ellie's shirt up so that it was under her arms, he freed her nut brown tits so that they sat provocatively on top of her bra.

His thin lips curled as they dived towards her, biting her rock hard nipples and sucking her breasts until she cried out, forcing him to use a hand to gag her. Ellie bit into his skin, making him snarl and increase his greedy attack on her chest.

Stepping as far back as he could in the confined space, he released his stiff shaft from his suit trousers. Ellie watched in morbid fascination as he ignored her obvious need and spunked all over her chewed tits.

Stopping to wipe his cock on one of the cleaner's cloths, he smiled sarcastically at Ellie, and passed her a jumbo sized glue stick from the shelf. 'I'd work myself off on that if I were you sweetheart.' He spoke bluntly as he stared into her flushed face, 'Oh, and do clean yourself up before you come back to work. You look a total mess.'

CHAPTER EIGHTEEN

Some people like it straight, some kinky, some meek, and some revel in taking charge. Others like rough. Sometimes very very rough, almost torturous in fact.

The wine bar was fairly quiet. It was too early to be heaving with club-goers and too late to have after hours office workers clogging up the bar. I was sat having a drink with a friend, when we began to tune into a conversation at the next table.

The girl, who we later learnt was called Clare, was chatting to another, who was almost continuously rubbing at her shirt covered wrists. After getting the gist of their discussion, my friend persuaded me to go and introduce myself. With her companion's permission, Clare told us their story.

Dark Knight

Paul's voice was softly spoken. 'Heather's always had this medieval, castle, forest, thing going on. Not in a romantic way. There's no room in her mind for chivalrous knights coming to whisk her away to make passionate love in a flowery glade.

No, her medieval fantasy is Thomas Malory turned on its head. Twisted, made darker, colder and, well… real.'

'Is that why she works here then? To get closer to a sexual fantasy?'

'Oh yes.' Paul looked at Clare, his grey eyes fixed onto her own. 'We have an agreement in that area, Heather and I.'

Clare pulled her dark red cloak tighter around her shoulders. Something about his gaze made her feel cold, as if he could see right into her soul. 'An agreement?'

'Yes.' Pulling the hood of his own black cloak over his closely cropped twenty-first century haircut, Paul stood up from his pseudo-medieval chair in the banqueting hall. 'I would like some help, if you're interested?'

Clare didn't reply, but her curiosity was intense. Heather was so withdrawn; a haughty dignity surrounded her petite frame, and her air of contempt for the falsely sanitised view of medieval life they offered the tourists that flocked to the fourteenth-century manor, where they all worked as historical figures, both infuriated and intrigued her.

Standing, Clare followed Paul into the now deserted grounds. 'I think you should tell me what this agreement with Heather is all about. Exactly what help you require.'

The summer evening felt warmer now they'd left the draughty hall and Paul removed his cloak completely, revealing his leather hose, boots and faded white shirt. 'I will tell you everything, but ONLY if you agree to help me.'

Clare felt a prickle of apprehension and excitement, how could she refuse him? She had wanted Paul for so long, dreamt about him in the quiet night of her bedroom, but he only seemed to have eyes for Heather. Perhaps he had noticed her after all. Clare sat next to Paul on the grass verge that surrounded the house, and had a sudden feeling that somehow he knew everything, her deepest secrets and desires, even those things she didn't know about herself.

For years she'd wanted this. Dreamt it. Needed it. Now, with reality so close, Heather's mind wrestled with her already aroused body. *Did she really want to do this?*

The overhead clang of an iron gate put an abrupt end to her thoughts. There was no chance of backing out now as she waited in the dank dark. Approaching footsteps resounded down the spiralled stone staircase. The eerie air of the past felt damp against her goose pimpled skin. Her hands bound in front of her, Heather's rough green tunic was dirty from her imprisonment in the manor's cellar, far below ground level, where lichens and mosses covered the walls with a slimy soft cushion.

As the footfalls of her Lord got closer, Heather's breathing quickened with anticipation, making her breasts tighten beneath the scratchy Hessian material. It rubbed against her unbound tits, causing her already hard nipples to chafe.

The cellar, not included in the tourist trail, was usually completely empty, but now a narrow wooden table was positioned along one wall. It was covered in a variety of unlit candles, and beneath it sat a box of equipment. She had wanted this so badly, and Paul had agreed to help, but on one condition.

Heather had hesitated when he'd first suggested an additional element, a surprise. Whilst it was her fantasy, no matter how depraved things got, it was still within her control. An unknown factor however, that changed things. He'd insisted though, claiming it would make the experience even better. Heather hadn't been so sure, but had eventually agreed. Ever since then, her mind had revolved around what Paul's extra little something might be.

Heather heard a creak of wood. The door slowly opened, and the room was invaded with a wide beam of light, which stung her gloom adjusted eyes.

Paul came in, his cloak wrapped around his naked form, his hood up. Without acknowledging his prisoner, he used the candle he held to ignite the others. Light swept through the cellar and the aroma of warming beeswax pervaded the atmosphere. Only then did he turn to Heather. Paul approached in two swift strides. Grasping hold of her stubby ginger pony tail, he dragged her towards the table, causing her bare feet to stumble against the rough stone floor.

'Kneel.' He wasn't Paul in here, her friend, her confident and occasional lover. He was her Lord and Master, and Heather was quick to obey as her knees hit the ground.

He grabbed her chin and jerked her head up. 'You were caught pleasuring yourself girl. That's a sin. Punishment, severe punishment is required. Yes?'

107

'Yes my Lord.' Heather lowered her eyes respectfully, but her nipples hardened further and her pussy pulsated as her fantasy stretched out before her.

He undid her wrists and yanked the tunic over her head. Already cold, Heather's teeth began to chatter as her naked flesh lost its only layer of protection. Paul picked a long rough rope from the box beneath the table. 'Bend.'

Standing briefly before placing her hands onto her knees, the inevitable lash forced a scream from her lips. Paul aimed and struck again and again, until her small pale arse was hot and red, and tears streaked down her small face.

'That'll warm you up. Now stand.'

Heather's legs felt unsteady as she rose. The blood that had rushed to her head, eased back through her body. She tensed as he began to tease the end of the rope against her teats. Despite the beating she'd just endured, Heather couldn't prevent the moan of lust that escaped her lips as he toyed with her tits.

She regretted her lapse in concentration straight away as he pulled a dirty cloth from his pocket and stuffed it firmly between her teeth. As Heather acclimatised herself to the lack of movement in her jaw, Paul carefully began to loop the long rope around her.

Circling one globe, then crossing the ropes and encircling the other, Paul harnessed her chest swiftly and effectively. Pulling the two loose ends around her back, he ran them down and then up between her legs, using them to ease apart her nether lips, before tucking the long ends up through her breast's undersides. Heather shifted uncomfortably, thankful that the ropes weren't as tight in reality as her imagination had made them.

As if sensing her relief, Paul jerked the two ends of rope, making the harness immediately body-hugging. Heather gasped into her gag as the prickly hemp dug into her skin. 'Any infraction and I will pull them even tighter. Yes?'

Unable to reply vocally, Heather inclined her head, aware that the tears which had dried onto her face were threatening again.

Paul dropped the rope and stood back to admire his work. Dejected, humiliated, delicious. Heather cowered before him. He felt power course through his body. Pushing his captive back against the far wall to where, hundreds of years before, metal hooks had been placed high on the walls to hang cured wild fowl before it was prepared for the Lord's table, Paul tied thick cord around each of Heather's wrists. Elongating her arms high above her head, he attached her wrists to conveniently spaced hooks, forcing her to stand on her tip-toes, stretching every muscle in her legs, back and arms.

So far Paul had followed Heather's instructions to the letter, and was making her submissive fantasy a living and wonderfully painful reality. Now though, things were more uncertain. Her instructions had been simple; punishment, humiliation, bondage and beating. A total contrast to the normal behaviour of a person who was usually so sure of herself, so much in control. Now, having already received all those things, Heather's brain teamed with a multitude of possibilities as she pondered what her Lord would do next.

Paul knew precisely what he wanted to do to this fascinating creature. He wanted to see just how much this woman could take. He picked up a candle from the table and, holding it briefly in front of her wide blinking eyes, began to tease the orange flame inches away from her chest.

Mindful of the possibility of, not just her rope harness, but her skin burning, Heather wriggled, attempting to back into the solid wall behind her. Paul laughed and moved the heat closer still so that the shadows of flickering warmth danced across her imprisoned flesh.

As he watched, her right nipple began to pucker in the intense heat, and sweat broke out on her neck and chest. Paul moved the candle to the other breast, causing Heather to bite down hard into her gag, her frightened eyes never daring to stray from the spluttering wick.

Paul lowered himself to his knees and angled Heather's legs as wide apart as her stretched limbs could go. Then, using the candle light as a guide, he began to examine the folds of her shaved pussy with his thick fingers.

Heather's moans, caused by both his touch and her discomfort, were stifled by her material restraint. Every stretched muscle across her body stiffened, as her Lord focused the heat onto her triangle.

Paul, keeping the flame as close as possible to her cunt, began to blow softly against her vulnerable flesh. Heather leapt within her bonds as, for a fraction of a second his soft breath brushed the flame onto her skin. Paul smiled beneath the shadow of his cloak as he did it again, and then again, each time making the flame glance her skin for a little longer, until her sweet mound showed the first signs of being singed and Heathers jerking body made his task impossible.

'I never said you could move!' Paul's voice boomed out, echoing around the room. He yanked her rope harness hard, causing Heather to dribble around her cloth muzzle as it bit against her supple flesh.

Struggling to keep still, the throbbing in her arms increased, as she dangled before him. It was then, as he moved, that Paul's hard cock peeked invitingly out of the dark folds of material. Heather looked at it hungrily, and felt her juice leak down her still outstretched legs, soaking the ropes and her thighs. Paul had gone far beyond the realms of her fantasy already, and her body, although shocked, sore, and aching in pain, felt hopelessly, wonderfully, turned on by its total submission and his unquestioning control.

Paul saw the thin liquid seep from her. 'You utter whore. How dare you allow this to excite you! I should leave you here to rot.' He turned and headed towards the solid wooden door, and with a final glance at Heather's petite tortured body, left the cellar, slamming the door behind him.

Heather stared after him. This wasn't part of the plan. All he was supposed to do now was kiss her, let her down and make love to her. Okay, the candle thing had been unexpected, but then he'd said he was going to add something extra to her plans. Surely he hadn't just left? He was just playing with her some more, he'd be back. As the seconds passed though and the door didn't open, Heather closed her legs in a hopeless attempt to become more comfortable and tried to control the panic that had begun to build in her gullet.

Now she could truly begin to comprehend the horror and all consuming fear the medieval prisoner must have experienced as they were trussed up and left alone, and this wasn't even a real dungeon. Her arms felt as though they were about to separate from their sockets and numbness began to infuse her legs.

The guttering of the candles made sinister shadows dance around the walls, but they were too far away to provide her any warmth, and her body, that had been singed only minutes before, felt damp and cold. An unstoppable shivering engulfed her. Yet, to her shame, Heather still felt herself craving Paul's firm touch as the harness continued to pinch her tender breasts and tease her pussy. She shut her eyes, and tried to focus her mind on her Lord's return.

Clare had been sat on the other side of the cellar door. She longed to see what Paul had done to Heather, if he really had carried out their agreement as planned, but mindful of Paul's warning of consequences, Clare refrained from spying. Her imagination however, had filled in the blanks as she listened in excited horror to the cries that had escaped beneath the cellar's door and her own body, naked beneath her cloak, was experiencing its own desperate requirements.

At last Paul came from the room. Clare gasped at the sight of his protruding dick as he, pulling her up roughly, pushed against her, crushing her mouth with his own in a frustrated rush of lust.

When he finally pulled away and she'd caught her breath Clare asked, 'Is all well my Lord?' She curtsied as she spoke, unsure if his role as Lord was continuing outside of Heather's prison.

'Excellently,' Paul looked at her with hungry wolf like eyes, and thrust a hand between her legs. He rubbed his whole palm against her clit, producing the fastest orgasm of Clare's life.

'We will continue as planned, and you will assist.' It wasn't a question.

Paul opened Clare's cloak wider, and began to suck on her left teat. 'Yes Master, with pleasure.'

Paul turned his attention to her other breast, but all the time his mind was on the small girl hanging like a cur in the next room. His head was littered with pictures of Heather's harnessed tits, which eagerly invited a tongue to cool them. First though, he needed to warm them up.

It had only been ten minutes, but to Heather, Paul's absence felt hours long. When she heard the door reopening, it was an effort to raise her head, but when she did she blinked in horror. He'd promised her! He'd promised that this was their secret, that no one else would know. No one! Yet there was a woman, not just a woman but Clare! Clare, who simpered and smiled her way through the day. Clare, who really did seem to believe that medieval life was all holy days, hearts and flowers. Clare, who spoke to the tourists with a frighteningly confident lack of knowledge. Beautiful, tall, dark, and oddly captivating, Clare.

Paul tilted Heather's chin up and pulled out her gag. 'As you can see, I have a helper. What do you think of my little extra something?'

Heather's eyes glared at him angrily, but she said nothing as she slowly digested the fact that the candle hadn't been his additional surprise after all.

Paul's brow creased. 'I believe the correct response is "Yes my Lord, Thank you my Lord."'

To emphasise his point, Paul pulled her harness hard, until Heather's eyes watered and she had no choice but to blurt out, 'Yes Sir. Thank you my Lord.'

Paul let go of the ropes, replaced the soaking gag, and took a step backwards. 'That's better. Now, I see you are cold. Let's warm you up a bit shall we.'

Heather barely had time to compose herself as Paul picked up a short twig from beneath the table. She tensed as the first blow landed on her secured and forcibly pert breasts. The cloth muffled her squeals, as hot waves of agony shot through her delicate teats. After spending some time concentrating on one side, Paul continued to ignore her pain, and adjusted his position so he could work his way over Heather's other tit.

All the time Clare watched in amazement. This was way beyond the image she'd concocted in her mind. She couldn't drag her eyes from Heather. Her alabaster skin was streaked with grime, bruised from Paul's attentions, shivering with cold, and yet flushed with heat from the latest assault. Clare's body was suddenly inflamed with an unfamiliar desire to touch Heather, to kiss her better, to take her from Paul's torture and caresses her, sooth her, and tend to her. She was surprised; this was not the reaction she'd expected, but a nagging voice at the back of her mind told her that it was exactly the reaction Paul had expected.

Paul dropped the twig. 'You'd like me to kiss you better now wouldn't you?'

Heather nodded fervently.

'Well, I'm sorry to disappoint you, but that's not going to happen.' He beckoned to Clare to approach him.

She moved quickly to his side, letting her cloak fall to the floor, revealing her tall slim darkly tanned body. With no hesitation, Paul leant forward and began to suckle and lick Clare's right nipple.

Heather's mouth, dry and sticky, clenched around the cloth, her eyes were bright with tears of desperation. That was her attention, that was what she needed, it was hers by right.

Paul looked up at Heather, 'You look a mess!' Then he turned to Clare's left breast, licking and nibbling at her nipple until she began to sway and rock against him.

Heather could only watch as her Master stared back at her. 'Everything you crave I shall give to Clare.' Paul kept his eyes on Heather for a split second longer, and then turned back to Clare, kissing her deeply, running his tongue around her mouth, and wrapping her inside his cloak to provide her chilled flesh some warmth. Then he turned Clare round and, pushing her to the floor, climbed on top of her so he could jam his stiff cock into her wet opening in full view of his prisoner.

Hot jealousy whipped through Heather. She no longer cared if he punished her further. After all, what else could he do? She closed her eyes, but that alone was not enough to block out what was happening before her as Clare began to mewl gently and Paul's grunts of satisfaction filled the room.

She'd wanted humiliation, well she'd got it. Heather opened her eyes again, facing the fact that her fantasy had gotten away from her. Yet, in that moment of realisation, she felt an erotic thrill shoot through her like no other. This was something even darker than her dreams, something vicious, something... better.

As he pumped his load into Clare, Paul held her closely, lovingly almost, but continued to watch Heather all the time. He had seen the betraying glimmer of renewed longing, of bizarre black satisfaction in her green eyes and understood it. Moving away, Paul wrapped himself back into his cloak, helped Clare to stand and pointed to the table. She nodded, concentrating hard on walking in a straight line, her legs weak from his fucking. Picking up the slimmest candle, Clare took it to her Master.

The flame streamed out as Paul carried it towards Heather. Lifting it up to her hands, he held the candle next to her right wrist and began to burn through the cord. Heather's heart pounded in her chest as she braced herself. Her scream shot through her gag as the flame burnt into her skin before snapping the cord, allowing her right arm to drop like lead with an agonising crack of her shoulder blade.

Clare winced as Paul began to free the other arm. It was hard not to retch as the cellar filled with the odour of burning rope and flesh.

Once she was loose, Heather's knees sagged and she fell to the ground, rubbing her wrists fiercely.

'Sit up!' Making no concession for her fragile state, Paul barked at her.

Heather, slowly, very slowly, dragged herself up into as much of a sitting position as she could manage. Clare had to physically restrain herself from helping, from running to Heather's crumpled form. It was a pitiful sight, but Paul looked so strong, so determined, that she daren't move.

After leaving Heather sprawled for a few minutes, Paul gestured to Clare, who moved eagerly forward and knelt between Heather's legs. Slowly, and with the greatest care, Clare eased the ropes around Heather's pussy a little and with a combination of urgent longing and apprehension of the unknown, began to kiss the hard slick nub.

Heather's body, assaulted, bound and abused, shook in an instant ecstasy which was both sudden and violent in its intensity.

Paul looked down at the girls, both enjoying a new and unexpected intimacy, as Clare, with a nod of approval from her Lord, began to caress the encased breasts, wrap Heather's flesh in her own, and ease the sodden cloth from her mouth.

Paul's eyes gleamed with renewed longing and admiration as Heather, despite all that had gone before, found the strength to reciprocate, and attack Clare's mouth with greedy pleasure. His cock, hard again, vibrated before him as he watched the rivals of the past writhe together on the filthy gravel floor. Taking his penis between his hands, he stood over them and, increasing his grip, pulled at himself until he showered his sticky load over the medieval waifs now totally oblivious to his existence.

He left them then. Together in the dirt, one having fulfilled the fantasy of a life time, the other experiencing a fantasy she hadn't even realised she'd had.

CHAPTER NINETEEN

When you start frequenting the night spots of Britain's major cities, you quickly realise that collecting erotic stories is tame compared to the activities of those who get their kicks from amassing the actual experiences themselves.

When these connoisseurs set their sights on someone, they rarely give up until their conquest is complete.

Introduced to me by a friend of a friend of a client of Kit's, the owner of this story obliged my request to speak into my dictaphone.

Van

'He stood about 6 ft 6ins tall, probably because his boots were so chunky. Without them I guessed he'd be a bit shorter, but his sheer bulk meant he'd still look like a giant. His ginger hair was cut tight into the back of his neck, but was thicker at the front and sides. As with many ginger-haired folk, his face was bespeckled with freckles. I decided to make it my mission to find out if he had freckles anywhere else.

They were laughing, chatting together, all four of them propped against the bar, giving the impression that it would take a meteor to move them. I felt restless as I watched them. It had been ages since my last fuck and I was horny to the point of desperation. He already seemed a challenge; a mountain I had to climb.

I kept staring at him, until eventually he looked in my direction and I managed to catch his eye. I did a half smile and turned away at the same time. It was classic stuff really, but it was enough to make sure he'd look at me again.

I'd known they were in there, not only because I'd got used to their routine over the past week, but because today their van was parked directly outside the pub.

Physical jobs. I've always been attracted to men in manual employment. It's something about all those dirty clothes and tool belts; as if they are always ready to tackle any situation, any task.

Removal men were a bit of a diversion really, but the thought of all that strength qualified them for my attention. No wimp could get a solid wooden double wardrobe up a staircase without pausing for breath.

They were still talking, but I knew I had caught his attention, so I headed up to the bar to get another drink, standing as close to the group as possible. They were laughing about their latest job, something about an aquarium. Just before I turned my back on them with drink in hand, I looked directly into his eye, nodded and sat back down; trying to concentrate on the newspaper I'd bought with me.

About twenty minutes later I got up and headed for the door. I gave him one last glance (making very sure he saw it), and left, hoping I'd given him enough to piqué his curiosity as well as his groin.

I'd got about 100 yards down the road before I heard footsteps behind me. I didn't turn. I knew it was him. I could smell hard work on him; sweat, dust and beer.

A large hand caught my shoulder and turned me round. He was about to speak when I put a finger to his lips and shook my head. I hadn't been after a cosy chat.

He nodded and simply cast his arms around as if to ask 'where?'

I gestured to the van. Inclining his head, he pulled the keys out of his pocket and dragged me along after him, his urgency appearing as hot as mine.

He undid the back doors of the box van and almost threw me in. He really was as massively strong as I had fantasised. Not fat, but big and hard and toned. My mouth almost watered at what was about to happen.

Banging the doors shut behind us, we found ourselves in almost total darkness, with just our silhouettes visible in the gloom. We stood on an uneven pile of the rugs and sheets they used to cover clients furniture. We knew we didn't have long, his mates would be out soon; unless they had been told to wait, I didn't know. I didn't care.

His shirt was already off, his jeans and boxers followed. As my eyes became accustomed to the shadows, I drew a sharp breath as his dick jumped to attention. He looked determined, menacing even, and I was quickly aware I would have to let this man be in charge, and freely do whatever he wanted. For a fleeting second I wondered if I had finally bitten off more that I could chew, yet my body had already taken over, and I knew I would go wherever this new experience took me.

He roughly pulled me closer and dragged my t-shirt over my head, leaving my bare chest to shiver against the van's dank atmosphere. Then, forcing me to my knees, he offered his shaft to my mouth. I took it without hesitation. It almost filled my throat, forcing me to choke a little as I accommodated its width and length. He tasted both salty and sticky; this man worked hard, and now he was playing hard, and I was on the receiving end.

He increased his pace, thrusting into my mouth faster and faster, his fingers twisting tightly into my neatly cropped hair. Just as I thought he'd spill into my mouth he withdrew, placed a massive hand on the small of my back, and pinned me face down against the uneven surface.

I felt hasty fingers undo my belt and yank my jeans and underwear down just enough to reveal my small, taut, backside. The stale air brushed my skin briefly before I felt my own belt crack down. I howled out at the unexpected pain. He struck me twice more before he let out a groan of impatience; the first sign that he was enjoying himself as much as I was.

He hoisted my arse up towards him, as if my body weighed nothing at all. I heard the rip of a packet as he hastily pushed on a condom. A gob full of spit was smeared over his length as lube, and, after an initial probe with the end of his cock, he rammed himself inside my arse.

I really hope that van was sound proofed, as boy did I yell. He was just so fucking thick, I thought I'd split in half. I could feel his orgasm build as he increased his speed, drumming my body against him, until he finally let out an ogre's roar, spunking into me like a machine before dropping my unsatisfied body to the floor.

I lay there for a few seconds, gulping in deep breaths. Then he knelt next to me. 'Let's sort you out,' he spoke kindly, revealing the gentle nature which lay beneath that giant body. He cupped my own penis in his fist, and firmly brought me to my own blissful end.

We said nothing to else to each other. I left first, walking home triumphant.

It wasn't until later that I realised I never did find out about the extent of his freckles.'

CHAPTER TWENTY

Of course, you don't need company to have a story to tell, just a very fertile imagination…

Alone

The image was so strong that she was sure if she reached out her hand she would feel firm flesh ripple beneath her fingers.

The blindfold she'd secured around her own face blackened the room, but her eyes were tightly shut anyway. Her fingers lingered teasingly on the lace trim around her knickers.

In her mind she saw them; the strong hands which had her waist held firmly in their strong grasp. They were tanned and rough from hard outside labour; the nails scratched her skin as the fingers slipped inside her waistband.

Her own fingers traced the echo of her imagination as the lacy fabric was gradually eased down. She lay back on the bed, spreading her pale smooth legs wide for her invisible companion.

In the shadow of her thoughts, he moved forward, towering over her prone body. He picked up her hands and placed them on her firm breasts, ordering her to rub her nipples between her fingers.

She did as she was bidden, pinching her nut brown tips and rolling them between her palms. He had told her to be silent, but she was unable to comply. A sigh of satisfaction escaped from between her lips. He was pleased she had disobeyed; now he could punish her. Pushing a hairbrush into her hand, he ordered her to smack her right thigh with its back, before placing her left thumb into her slightly open mouth.

As she struck herself with the oval brush head she deflected the pain by concentrating on her thumb, treating it as though it was his firm dick. Licking, sucking and nipping. In the darkness he knocked her hand out of the way and replaced it with his thick shaft. Her tongue caressed its tip while she continued to assault her own leg.

He pulled out; her thumb made a small slurping noise as it followed suit. She ran the wet digit across her bare chest, forcing a squeak of pleasure from her lips at the damp touch on her hard inflamed nipples.

Her leg was burning as she dropped the brush. Behind her mask he kissed her sore thigh. He whispered in her ear, and she obeyed. Her slender fingers fished around in the cool glass of gin and tonic she'd placed next to her bed. She extracted an ice cube. Her body jumped as stray droplets of alcohol and mixer melted into her. For a second she lost her concentration, what she was about to do might just be too much. No, she could see him watching, waiting for her to act.

The ice cube was starting to melt in her hand. She rubbed it over the fast bruising thigh and gasped as sheer cold coursed through her. Her breath became shallow and her mouth felt suddenly dry as she started to stroke herself between her legs, slowly trailing her fingers so they circled but never touched her clit. She removed the cube from her leg and placed it on her overheated chest, causing herself to cry out in blessed agony as the chill swept through her tits, whilst her other hand continued to warm her pussy.

She swapped actions, pushing the ice cube against her neglected clit and pinching her right nipple. She cried out anew into the vacant room as the slowly nurtured waves of desire became stronger.

In the dark he was watching, his hand on his cock, leisurely gliding it up and down as he enjoyed the spectacle before him.

The ice cube had halved in size. She pushed its remains into her pussy's hungry mouth. It was the final touch as her body spasmed and bucked against the bed.

Beneath the blackness of the blindfold he came, shooting his load across her chest, her body twisting as her imagination brought them both to a satisfied silence.

EPILOGUE

If I have learnt anything from putting together this collection, it's that you cannot tell what someone is into by just looking at them.

The dominatrix is not always young, slim and basque bound. Submissives don't naturally cower, and can be found hidden within the strongest personality. Anal exploration is not just the province of the gay community, and far more of us are bi-sexual than society is yet ready to admit. You don't have to be beautiful or thin to be attractive, and you should never ever assume that the ordinary looking forty-something couple in the street only do it missionary style.

The gambit of sexual experience within the bounds of this small country, indeed, within the bounds of the English Home Counties alone, is wide indeed.

I have collected stories that are shocking, touching and arousing.

Am I always convinced that the tales I hear are true? Are they embellished or exaggerated? Perhaps, although I pride myself on the care I take, and the large number of tales that didn't make it into this book are (hopefully), the ones I suspect of being more than a little over-told by their protagonists. I willingly admit however, that in those cases where I have simply overheard a conversation, there are frequently gaps I have used my own imagination to fill.

I shall leave you now, and head off to continue my search. The fantasies of the British public are just waiting for me to find them. I'll head to Scotland first I think, then maybe Devon and Cornwall, possibly Wales... I'm the one with the chestnut hair and the half smile. The female with the brightly coloured notebook and a slim black roller pen in the corner of a coffee shop, on the back seat of a bus, or sat on a stool at the edge of the club bar.

I'll see you there...